Boundary Waters Boy

ALEC BOOSTROM'S PIONEER LIFE
IN THE CANOE COUNTRY

Jack Blackwell

ISBN-13: 978-0-9740207-9-2

Printed in the United States

10 9 8 7 6 5 4 3 2

Produced By
Northern Wilds Media, Inc.
Grand Marais, MN
www.northernwilds.com

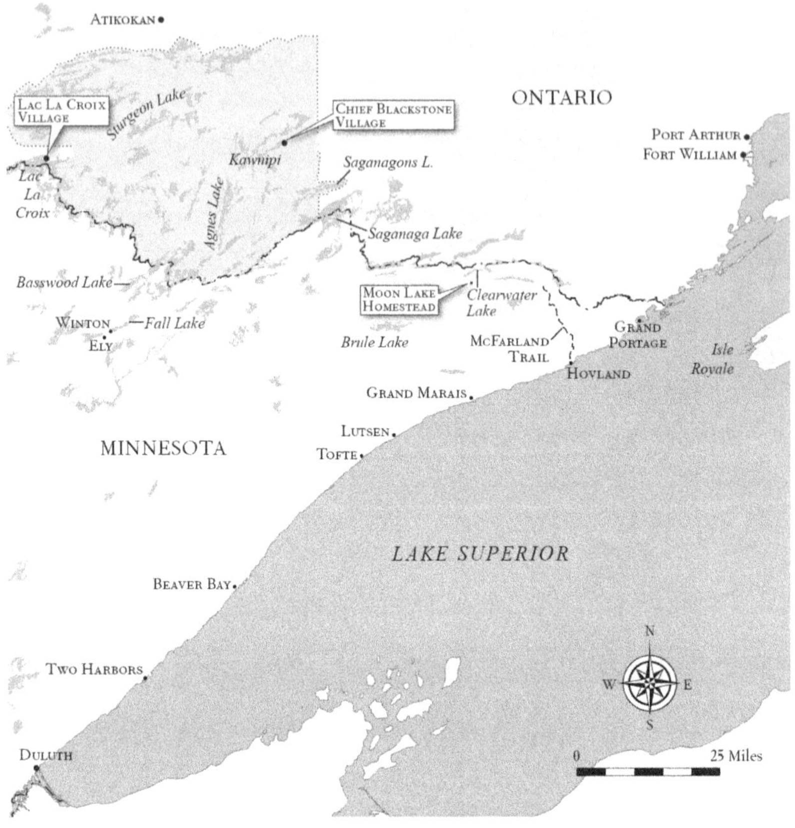
ATIKOKAN
ONTARIO
Lac La Croix Village
Sturgeon Lake
CHIEF BLACKSTONE VILLAGE
PORT ARTHUR
FORT WILLIAM
Kawnipi
Saganagons L.
Lac La Croix
Agnes Lake
Saganaga Lake
Basswood Lake
Moon Lake Homestead
Clearwater Lake
WINTON
Fall Lake
Brule Lake
McFARLAND TRAIL
GRAND PORTAGE
Isle Royale
ELY
HOVLAND
GRAND MARAIS
LUTSEN
TOFTE
MINNESOTA
LAKE SUPERIOR
BEAVER BAY
N
W E
S
TWO HARBORS
DULUTH
0
25 Miles

INTRODUCTION BY STUART OSTHOFF

My wife, Michelle, and I are the publishers of the *Boundary Waters Journal* (BWJ), a quarterly publication about the Boundary Waters Canoe Area Wilderness. As BWJ publisher for the past twenty-eight years, I have read nearly everything ever written on the BWCAW, and I must say, *Boundary Waters Boy* is the best historical account I have ever seen about this area. I am certain readers will be captivated by this very personal account of both the hardships and rewards of living in the Boundary Waters.

FORWARD

The Boundary Waters Canoe Area Wilderness (BWCAW) in northeastern Minnesota has for many years been the most heavily-visited of all the wilderness areas in the United States. What helps make this wilderness the national leader is the outstanding beauty of a vast million-acre network of inter-connected lakes and streams. Visitors travel by canoe during the summer, or snowshoe during the winter, over a seemingly endless possibility of routes. They experience a landscape similar to what the first white visitors encountered centuries earlier.

In spite of its popularity, there are outstanding opportunities for solitude, just as the 1964 Wilderness Act promised. Fish are plentiful in the lakes. Wolves, moose, bear, beaver, loons and many other animals abound. It is truly impressive.

The million-acre Quetico Provincial Park in Ontario is a companion wilderness. It shares the common international boundary between these two amazing wilderness areas. It is possible to travel by canoe from here all the way to Hudson's Bay in northern Canada.

A few small towns are located near the edge of the wilderness. The area's residents have always had to work hard and be creative to make a living. That includes guiding, trapping, hunting and fishing in the wilderness and recreation, logging and many other activities outside.

People so love this area that many of them continue to return each year for as long as they are able. Others are so attracted to the area that they move here permanently. Still others have remained for multiple generations and their family names are well-known. What they all have in common is an emotional attachment to this region. They may explain it in many different ways, but to them there is no other place like it.

But what is the history of this spectacular area? How did it come to be what it is today? Who were some of the early visitors? What did they encounter? What was life like in the surrounding towns? How about the Indians? Where were they and how did they live?

The experiences of one man who came here in 1914, fifty years prior to the original Wilderness Act, help us understand. His stories, told in his own words, are the historical report of an insider. It is an account that teaches us this area's history, its seasons, its animals, and its people. Both experienced locals and visitors will learn valuable new information from these narratives.

These stories were told to me by my grandfather, Alec Boostrom, prior to the time of his death in 1967. Good historical records exist from this period and provided additional details. They are in the list of historical records in the back of the book. In addition, my mother, Jean, has a good memory of her early life and was very helpful. My sister, Mary, and my brother, Billy, remember stories from our grandfather and contributed. Billy is a respected elder who lives on the Grand Portage Indian Reservation. He is also active in the Medewiwin religion and helped with many of the Indian subjects.

I have carefully researched the accuracy of the stories. In addition I had drafts reviewed by numerous people. Several local residents who knew my grandfather reviewed and contributed. The staff at the Cook County Historical Society reviewed and offered comments and pictures. One of their member's uncle was a trapping partner of Alec's. I spoke with Hoot Hautala's son, Jack, from Winton who offered comments and pictures about his father and reviewed the draft of Chapter 7. I tracked down Anne Cook Bowler-O'Shea, the daughter of Wesson Cook, the surveyor in charge of the US Geological Survey's border lakes project. Anne's mother was Rose Zimmerman Cook and Anne told me about both her mother and father. She also confirmed Rose Lake was named for her mother.

In my career with the US Forest Service I was fortunate at one point to be the Recreation and Wilderness Staff Officer for the Superior National Forest. In that capacity I was responsible for oversight of the BWCAW management and coordination with officials from Quetico Provincial Park. One of those officials was Shirley Peruniak, the Park Historian. Upon retirement she wrote a book called *QUETICO Provincial Park, An Illustrated History*. I drew upon it and also material from Justine Kerfoot's books and Bill Magie's book for information about Chief Blackstone. Betty Powell Skoog's book *A Life In Two Worlds* is also a wealth of information about Chief Blackstone and other events around the Quetico Park. Betty grew up on Saganagons Lake and is the daughter of Tempest Powell and granddaughter of Jack Powell and Mary Ottertail.

In 1991, the Province of Ontario issued a formal apology to the descendants of the Indian people of the Quetico, lending further credence to these earlier stories.

I arranged for Walter Caribou to speak to a meeting of the leadership of the Superior National Forest. He described the dramatic Windigo event and killing on Basswood Lake. Walter told the story in his own words. My brother was also there and we remembered Walter's story identically.

The Minnesota Conservation Volunteer magazines contain some excellent material on the early game wardens including Joe Bickner's accounts of Alec and Charlie Boostrom. Dr. Julius Wolff (deceased) was a history professor at the University of Minnesota, Duluth. He also produced some great publications of the early trappers, game wardens and forest fires.

I've taken time to share some of my research to demonstrate that I am confident this is an accurate portrayal of my grandfather's life. However, it should still be considered historical fiction.

Jack Blackwell

DEDICATION

This book is dedicated to my mother, Jean Boostrom Blackwell Roberts, who is also known as "Sister." Thank you for the wonderful job you did raising our family. I love you.

TABLE OF CONTENTS

CANADA
Arrow Lake
Mountain Lake
Moose Lake
Rose Lake
North Fowl Lake
Daniels Lake
Clearwater Lake
West Pike Lake
East Pike Lake
Royal River
South Fowl Lake
Caribou Lake
Pine Lake
Bearskin Lake
Moon Lake
Stump River
McFarland Lake
MOON LAKE HOMESTEAD
East Bearskin Lake
Alder Lake
Stump River
Crocodile Lake
Otter Lake
Greenwood Lake
McFARLAND TRAIL
UNITED STATES
Tom Lake
Irish Creek
Northern Light Lake
Hovland
Devil Track Lake
GRAND MARAIS
N
W E
S
LAKE SUPERIOR
0   5 Miles

1

Leaving Home

It was late September of 1914 in central Minnesota. I was the most excited I have ever been. I was leaving my family and the only home I had ever known for a whole new world in the wild country of far northern Minnesota. My older brother, Charlie, had gone up there near the Canadian border to explore in 1911. He had spent a good part of the next three years there while he trapped, hunted, fished, and learned about the country. Charlie had gone alone and had built a small log cabin at a place called Moon Lake, where he intended to homestead. He had saved some money, and now he had returned for his wife and infant son. He was going back for good this time.

I begged to go with them. Our Swedish immigrant parents must have realized there was no future for me on our small farm, because they agreed to let me go, if Charlie would take me. He said yes immediately. I was big and strong for my age, and I already knew how to hunt ducks and geese. With winter coming on, Charlie must have known he would need my help. I was fourteen years old, born in 1900, the last of five children—two boys and three girls. Charlie was second oldest; born ten years before me. I was proud to have completed the eighth grade.

The well-traveled road from Minneapolis to Duluth passes near Mille Lacs Lake. We came from Milaca on the southwest shore. We passed the towns of Moose Lake, Carlton, and a big one named Cloquet. We didn't know it then, but in a few years, we would hear of a terrible tragedy there. The road went down into the St. Louis River valley and on to the big Duluth harbor where the river empties into Lake Superior.

Charlie and I walked behind a wagon pulled by two horses

The steamer *America*. Cook County Historical Society

driven by a neighbor. Charlie's wife, Petra, and their month-old son, Donald, rode in the wagon. Also in the wagon were all our belongings, plus our food for the coming winter. This included fifty-pound sacks of flour and sugar. It was a fairly heavy load. We had two hundred pounds of flour, one hundred pounds of sugar, three bushels of beans, and other miscellaneous food, clothes, and camping gear. By the second day, we had reached Duluth.

Charlie led the way to the Booth Line steamship docks. The 180-foot steamer America was tied firmly to one of the docks. There were four large openings above the waterline on both sides of her hull. They were closed now. That night the neighbor and I slept under the wagon, while Charlie, Petra, and Donald slept in the wagon.

Early in the morning, the four dock-side doors were opened for loading, and men were busy adding cargo to her holds and deck. We unloaded the wagon in the dark and carried our supplies on board. Charlie paid our neighbor, and we all said goodbye.

There was seating for the three of us, but no cabin or bed. It didn't matter. We departed quickly, and by the end of the long day we were at our destination of Hovland. Our speed was impressive. One of the Booth Line crew members told us we were cruising at nineteen knots, or twenty-two miles per hour. The captain's name was John Smith. We learned he was an Indian from the Fond du Lac Reservation near Cloquet.

I was wide-eyed with amazement at the wild country we were passing. The beauty of the lake and the rugged coast with occasional lighthouses was awesome. The hills were covered with bright red, orange, and yellow hardwood trees, and deep green pines and spruce. I thought the falls back home were pretty, but this was even more beautiful. I have never lost my love for the beauty and the wonder of this land. Over the years, it has become even stronger.

During most of the winter, travel by boat along the coast was impossible. It would be months before new supplies could get through. There was mail service by dog team. It was easy to see how there could be no overland road along the steep and rocky coast.

It is 130 miles to Hovland. We followed the shoreline in a northeasterly direction. We docked at the port of Two Harbors, where I saw trains carrying iron ore from mines in the far north. Next it was on to Beaver Bay, Schroeder, Tofte, Lutsen, Grand Marais, then Hovland, where we disembarked. "Boat Day" brought many people down to the docks to meet us at each stop. There was always a lot of excitement with people coming and going. Someone's pet moose even showed up at the Grand Marais stop.

From Hovland, the America would continue to the Indian reservation and settlement at Grand Portage, located just south of the Canadian border. This place was named for the long portage from Lake Superior to the Pigeon River, including the lake and river route to the Canadian northwest. In the past, Grand Portage is where French Canadian voyageurs would annually meet their counterparts from Montreal, who traveled down the Great Lakes in big, forty-foot-long canoes. Around 1800, at the height of the fur trade, two thousand people would gather there.

Next, the boat would continue north to Port Arthur, Ontario. Then it was out to the big island in Lake Superior, Isle Royale, where it would drop off supplies and pick up fish from the Norwegian fishermen living there.

On her return, the America would stop offshore from fishermen's homes along the coast. Conditions permitting, groups of these hardworking men would row out in their wooden skiffs and deliver barrels of salted lake trout, herring, and whitefish for the markets in Duluth and cities to the south.

At Hovland, we said goodbye to the crew of the America, and carried our things off the dock. I was going to miss the boat and all the excitement it caused in the towns. For the next fourteen years she continued this duty. In June of 1928, the America struck a reef and sank off Washington Harbor on Isle Royale. It was a big loss to the entire region.

Charlie found a place to pitch our tent, and we put it up in the dark. While Petra fixed supper, he left to see someone he knew.

When Charlie returned, he said, "We're in luck. Martin Jacobsen will haul us up the McFarland Trail tomorrow. It's a twenty-mile trip. We should make it in one day. Let's hope it doesn't rain."

We were up early the next morning. Charlie had found some wood and had a fire going. Petra fixed breakfast. It would have been easy to burn the food in the thin, metal frying pan, but she expertly moved the pan around the top of the metal grate, keeping all parts of it at the right temperature. She prepared three stacks of pancakes, one for each of us. We Boostrom boys love our pancakes.

We broke camp. Charlie and I took the tent down, folded it, and put it back into its packsack. We could not afford many loose items, because once we got to McFarland Lake it all had to fit into the two canoes Charlie had left there. From then on, we would have to carry everything across the portages leading to Moon Lake. Everything had to fit in its place and be neat and well organized, Charlie explained.

There was no sign of Martin yet, and Charlie told me I was free to look around as long as I kept an eye out for a horse and wagon. A short distance down the shore, I met a man mending his fishing net on a large wooden drying rack. While he worked, I watched. After a while, he began to talk. He had a thick accent. He said his name was

Emil Eliasen, and he was a bachelor fisherman. He told us he'd come from Norway twenty-four years ago and settled here.

From Emil I learned the North Shore was being settled, very quickly, it seemed to him. He told me the town of Hovland was officially formed in 1894. He said the United States had made a treaty with the Chippewa Indians back in 1854. The treaty created reservations for the Indians and opened up the rest of northeastern Minnesota to homesteading. I could tell he was proud of all the growth.

"It was slow to get started, but look at it now," he said. "There are lots of people living along the shore. We have regular boat service. Before long, there will even be roads connecting the towns."

Emil said it was still wild and unpopulated back inland where we were going. He thought even there, change was coming. When I left him, I was more excited than ever. I could hardly wait to get up that McFarland Trail and on to Moon Lake.

Soon Martin Jacobsen showed up. He had his horse hooked to a small wagon.

"Let's load up and get going," was about all he said. We quickly did that, and off we went. Martin drove the wagon and Petra and Donald rode in the box with all of our supplies. Charlie and I walked behind. It was going to be a long day. I tried to take everything in as we walked along. Martin said there was a new logging camp in the area, but we didn't go past it. At first, the trail followed a stream called the Flute Reed River. Martin said there were brook trout and rainbows in it, and the same kinds of fish could be found in all the North Shore streams.

At first, the trees were mostly popple and birch. Years later, I learned that people elsewhere call popple trees aspen, but to us they are always popple. Sometimes we would see big pine and spruce trees. We hadn't seen any wildlife yet. After the first mile, there were no more homesteads. Soon the trail became steeper, and we began climbing what looked like a long ridge. We started to see maple trees, and Martin said the Indians from Grand Portage tapped them to make maple sugar. There were certainly no big hills like this where we had come from. The trail became muddy in spots, and once in a while Petra and Donald had to get off while we pushed the wagon. We were still making good time.

We finally topped the ridge and continued following the trail due north. Now, there were many big white pine trees. We came to a good-sized stream called Irish Creek. It was running high from recent rains. You could tell the floor of the wagon was going to get wet.

Charlie said, "Okay, everybody. I know we're going to get wet, but we can't take a chance of ruining our supplies. We are going to have to carry all this stuff across to keep it dry."

"Everybody" meant Charlie, Petra, and me. Martin sat on the wagon, holding Donald while we carried our packsacks and bundles across. Once that was done and Petra had retrieved Donald, Martin drove the horse into the water. We knew the stream bottom was hard, and the wagon bounced across. The wagon floor went underwater at one point and we had to push it up the far bank. Now on the other side, we stopped for a break. We emptied our boots, wrung out our socks, and put our wet boots back on. Charlie went off into the woods and quickly came back with some dead sticks and poles. I was about to get my first canoe lesson.

"Alec," he said, "You'll learn when rain makes a canoe bottom wet, you have to put wood under your packs to keep the water from wicking up into them." With that said, he arranged the dry sticks and poles across the bottom of Martin's wet wagon bed and set our packs on top of them.

We started off again, still heading north. It was uncomfortable walking with wet feet, but I didn't complain. Being big and strong, I was doing my share. That Petra was something else. She always did more than her share of the work, while also taking care of Donald. She and Charlie were already a great team.

Later, we crossed one more stream called the Stump River. By late afternoon we arrived at McFarland Lake. There were some log cabins. Charlie's two canvas canoes were right where he had left them two months earlier. In those days, people never bothered someone else's property. Martin wanted to get started back right away, and so

Charlie paid him. We thanked him and he left us.

Charlie knew the owner of one of the cabins and had permission to use it. We pulled out what we would need for overnight, and piled everything else down near the lakeshore. We turned each canoe upside down, and lifted them over the piles so the canoes would keep everything dry if it rained. Petra made us rice and raisins for supper. Donald was well behaved and was no problem for her. We were all anxious to get moving.

That evening, Charlie told us some of the history of McFarland Lake. It was named after John McFarland, who had come here to stake a stone and timber claim. Instead, he found traces of gold, and sunk a shaft some distance from the lake. The gold appraised at only five dollars per ton. Unwilling to give up, McFarland brought in heavy mining equipment, but he soon ran out of money. He sold shares in his mine to John Gustafson and Adolph Carlson. With their help, the shaft was made deeper. Now the gold appraised at ten dollars per ton. They went deeper still, and the value of the gold increased again. However, they were below the lake level and the shaft flooded. McFarland was bankrupt and the others were out of money, too. McFarland became a schoolteacher in Grand Portage, and with his small salary bought groceries for Gustafson and Carlson, who kept looking for a rich vein of gold. They never found it. McFarland died in 1905, and is buried nearby.

Morning came quickly, and Petra fixed us another pancake breakfast. Then it was time to learn about canoes. I had been in a canoe once, duck hunting and trapping muskrats on Mille Lacs, but really didn't know much about them. Petra knew even less than I did. Charlie showed us how to properly load a canoe so the stern was slightly heavier than the bow. The only exception, he said, was if you are going down rapids. Then the bow should be heavier. He taught us to put the heaviest items on the floor to keep the canoe stable. He said to never load one top-heavy, or it would tip over easily. He told us not to get into a canoe until it is floating, because you might damage the bottom if you stepped into it while over a rock.

Without any fanfare, off we went. Petra and Donald rode in

Charlie Boostrom at Moon Lake cabin. *Note long paddles made from black ash.* BOOSTROM FAMILY PHOTO

Charlie's canoe. It had the biggest load and contained our most important supplies. I was alone in the second canoe, and my load was also a good one. At first, it seemed like I was heading all over the lake. I managed to keep it in the general direction I wanted to go by paddling on each side as necessary. I marveled at Charlie's ability to keep his going in a straight line while only paddling on one side.

Charlie brought his canoe alongside mine. "Alec, watch me paddle and I'll show you what we call the J-stroke." He brought his paddle down the side of his canoe in a powerful pulling stroke. This moved the canoe forward, but caused it to turn toward the opposite side. Instead of lifting his paddle out of the water, Charlie tilted it slightly up and brought it back while still in the water. This caused the canoe to return to where it had been pointed. The whole movement with the paddle resembled the letter J.

Charlie said, "Now you try it. Also, learn to paddle equally well on either side." Before long, I was doing better.

The outlet from McFarland is to the northeast, down the Royal River. Instead of heading there, Charlie led us northwest to the portage to Pine Lake. In later years, I learned from my Indian friends that the Royal River is named for the royal fern, a plant with special medicinal powers which is found there.

It took us two days to cover the five portages to Moon Lake. After all the beautiful country we had come through, I was a little disappointed at the lake's smaller size and general appearance. But Charlie's rough cabin looked good and it was a big relief to finally be "home." Petra took charge of the cabin, and we moved in. I was not comfortable staying inside with them at night, so I pitched the tent and slept outside for the time being.

We went to work immediately, cutting firewood for the winter and building another small cabin for me to sleep in and to store our extra provisions. It had no stove. Charlie pointed out in the event of a fire in the main cabin, this smaller one was our safety net. My sleeping bag was warm, plus I had the tent and extra clothing for insulation. I was happy, and could hardly wait for winter and trapping to begin.

2

My First Winter

Near the end of October, we had a good supply of firewood cut and stacked. The small cabin was done. We killed a moose, and stored the meat outside under a shelter we had built. We caught some northern pike in the lake. We worked from morning till night. Life was hard, but it was also good.

One day Charlie announced, "Alec, I think the mink are prime and it's time to start trapping. Let's find out for sure."

He brought two pieces of the northern pike we had caught, and we paddled over to the outlet of the lake. In the stream, he built a cubby from rocks and placed a small trap in the water in front of it. He anchored the trap to a green alder stick covered with other big rocks out in the running water.

He put half the fish in a bundle of leaves, and placed the bundle in the cubby. Charlie explained that the leaves kept birds from spotting and eating the fish. The cubby resembled a small, deep, open-top box, set on its side. There was only one way in. A mink had to come over the trap in the water to get to the bait. Farther down the creek, he made another cubby set with the other half of the fish.

He said, "Let's wait for two days and see if we catch anything."

I could hardly wait to go back. It seemed to take forever. When we returned, we found a nice dark mink in the first trap. It had drowned from the weight of the trap in the running water. Charlie took it and reset the trap. The second trap was just as we had left it.

We went back to the cabin yard and Charlie skinned the mink. He showed me how to determine if the fur was prime, which required a look at the inside skin. If it was black or mottled, he said it meant the guard hairs hadn't yet developed sufficiently, and the pelt was substandard. However, if the skin was white, it meant the fur was prime. Partially prime mink can still be sold. However, they receive a much lower price and it is always best to wait until their fur is in top condition. The weather had been cold, and this skin was white. Mink trapping could begin.

At first we used one of the canoes, and worked out in several directions from Moon Lake. I learned to read sign left by mink. They come out of the water to shit, and usually do it on top of a rock or log. It's black in color, maybe an inch long or more, and is about as thick as a lead pencil. By looking for this sign, you can tell if there are many mink in an area.

Soon the small ponds in quiet water developed "skim ice" overnight. It melted during the day, but Charlie knew our time of using the canoe was coming to an end. If skim ice remains for a second night, the resulting thickness is not possible to break with a paddle. Then travel by canoe is ended for the season.

Trapping is always hard on canoe paddles because they are used for more than paddling. Using a canoe around ice is even harder on them because you have to smash the ice with a paddle to break it and enable the canoe to move forward. Paddles are also used to temporarily hold a canoe in position by being jammed into the shallow lake bottom. We learned to carve our paddles from the clear wood in big white cedar trees. It's the strongest and lightest wood available. I always make their length to be from the ground to between a person's chin and nose, when standing upright. We made the handles thick and the blades narrow. This helped prolong their service life, but we still broke them regularly and had to carry spares.

Eventually, for trapping we had to switch to stronger, heavier paddles carved from the slow-growing, tight-grained black ash trees found in swamps. We made them a little longer than our regular cedar paddles. They worked well for breaking ice and the many other jobs our paddles had to do. These ash paddles lasted much longer, but were heavy compared to our cedar paddles. I've carved many paddles over the years, and still use the cedar type today.

Soon, we had to walk in the woods. We followed the shorelines and continued trapping the creeks. It was important to make sure there was running water over our traps, or they would freeze in the ice.

Our success with trapping mink dropped off as we covered less territory. Also, it seemed the mink no longer preferred our fish bait like they had earlier. We experimented, and discovered moose meat worked better. I guess their eating habits change as the weather gets colder.

We were told we could expect to see some caribou and we would have shot one for the meat if we came upon one. In a few years, they disappeared completely. However, more and more deer were showing up. There were also a few moose still around. Finding meat in the winter can be a real problem in this area, but fortunately we were well supplied with flour, beans, and rice.

The small lakes froze, and snow arrived. Before long, we were on snowshoes. Now our cubby sets were up on land, and we built them from dead wood and spruce or balsam boughs. We were after martin and fisher. We caught some. I learned to identify tracks and to further read sign left by animals. Travel by snowshoe became second nature, and once again we could cover longer distances.

Petra kept the home fires burning and always had something to eat for us when we returned. Sometimes it was fresh bread, and other times it was a big pot of soup or stew.

We were back at the cabin one afternoon when we had our first visitor. A tall, thin man snowshoed up to the yard. He appeared to be older than we were, and had a look of authority about him. He identified himself as Ed Mulligan. He said he was a county surveyor as well as a timber cruiser.

Charlie invited him inside. Petra served tea as we listened to Mr. Mulligan, who was very friendly. We learned that cruising timber meant getting the standing timber mapped, and determining how much of it there was. However, he explained, on this trip he was conducting survey business for the county. That included updating maps and noting the location of new arrivals, like us. He asked our names and noted them in the small diary he carried.

He talked about a subject that worried Charlie and Petra over the

Ed Mulligan cruising timber.
COOK COUNTY HISTORICAL SOCIETY

rest of the winter. Mr. Mulligan explained that we were located within a broad expanse of land called the Superior National Forest. It had been created by President Theodore Roosevelt in 1909. Prior to the creation of the national forest, this land had been closed to all homesteading.

Mr. Mulligan explained that he certainly had no authority to determine if we had legal title to our land, and said the county welcomed us with open arms. It would probably be a few more years, he thought, before the federal officials became organized and could deal with all of the remote settlers. Mr. Mulligan said Congress was considering a bill to allow everyone to stay on some kind of temporary basis. He said there were many of us in the same situation, and we shouldn't worry.

Charlie invited him to spend the night. Mr. Mulligan was prepared with a Woods Arctic eiderdown sleeping bag, and stayed with me in the small cabin. He left after breakfast the next morning, and promised to stop by later in the winter.

We went back to trapping, but that first encounter with Mr. Mulligan determined our fate at Moon Lake.

January turned to February, and we continued to catch some fur. By mid-February the wolves and foxes started to mate, and the country air was alive with their pungent odor. I had a birthday, and was now fifteen.

Ed Mulligan returned in February, and we had another nice visit with him. It was good to get news of what was happening in the outside world. Mr. Mulligan seemed to take a genuine interest in us and our welfare.

As the late winter sun climbed higher in the sky, I learned snow blindness can occur from the reflection of the sun on fresh snow. We wore smoked glasses to prevent the problem. I still always carry sun glasses in the late winter, and wear them as needed.

In March, we started trapping beaver through the ice. First, we had to find a live beaver house on a lake or pond. This was easy, because the beavers' body heat made some of the snow on top of the house melt. They stand out, if you know what to look for. Next, we located their cache of food for the winter they have stored near the house.

There are always one or two channels where beaver swim under the ice from their house to their cache. The ice is never very thick over these channels, and that is where we set our trap. After chiseling a hole through the ice, we attached a fresh piece of green popple, perpendicular to a dead pole. We built a small platform for the trap below this bait. Then we inserted the whole thing through the hole in the ice. This is called a "pole set." It is hard work. We caught a few big beaver using this method.

We learned to cook beaver meat, and we liked eating it. At first, we brought home some of the best-looking hind quarter meat. Petra cooked it, and we found it was very greasy. It didn't take Petra long to discover the best way to cook beaver is to parboil it first. I watched her bring the meat to a boil in a pot of water. She'd let it boil for five to ten minutes. A thick scum of grease formed on top of the water. She would pour this all off and then slice the meat. Next, she fried the slices in a frying pan. It is very good this way, and added variety to what we were eating. I still cook my beaver the same way.

By April, the days were getting longer, the weather was getting warmer, and the ground was beginning to thaw. I got to experience up close how the snow melts. It gets soft during the warm afternoons. When you step on it with snowshoes, the snow settles for up to a foot or more, sometimes in all directions.

The very wet, soft snow also sticks to your snowshoes. You need a stick or axe handle to tap on them to shake off the sticky snow. It becomes very difficult to walk any distance when this happens. One minute you are making great time on the frozen crust, and the next minute the crust has disappeared and you sink in deep. At night the snow freezes hard again, and the next day the cycle is repeated.

This also happens on the lakes, but then one day all the snow suddenly turns to water. Holes appear in the ice, and the ice starts to rise and the water drains into the holes. Small whirlpools appear, similar to what happens when you flush a toilet. This happens quite fast, usually in one afternoon. When complete, the snow and water are gone and we say the ice has "raised." For the next ten days or more, you can walk on the raised ice quite easily. The final stage is when it gets rotten and falls apart, usually from wind and waves.

By mid-April, open water appeared. We changed our trapping technique to open water sets, and we began to catch more beaver. When spring breakup ended, our trapping was done.

We had fur to sell. Charlie and I walked thirty-five miles to Grand Marais, where we sold it to Charlie Johnson at his trading post. Charlie built the trading post in 1898 after moving from his Rice Lake homestead north of Lutsen. Previously, he had hauled equipment to a place called the Paulson Mine by dog team during the winter and by heavy packs on foot during the summer. Charlie was a hard worker and a good businessman.

Charlie had quite a trading post there in Grand Marais. He had started small and was originally in competition with Henry Mayhew. Henry later sold to him, and now Charlie had a good-sized place with lots of merchandise that served the area's Indian and white trappers. The Indians liked Charlie, because they believed him to be honest and he took the time to learn their language. You could buy everything from salt pork to bear traps in his store. There was even a cracker barrel with free samples. I don't remember the exact prices, but we were very happy with the amount Charlie Johnson paid us for our fur, and we purchased more food and some clothing. We started right back after the trade. We were gone four days.

Over the winter, Charlie and Petra decided they were no longer certain they wanted to make their home at Moon Lake. They wanted to explore the country during the summer to see if they could find someplace better. Our time at Moon Lake had ended.

3

The International Border

From Ed Mulligan, we learned about the work of the International Boundary Commission. They had started marking the official boundary between the United States and Canada, beginning at Lake of the Woods in 1899. The job would be finished when they reached Lake Superior, which was estimated to be in 1918.

By now, they were working southeast from a big lake named Lac La Croix to two other big lakes named Crooked and Basswood. They were headquartered in Ely and would be coming this way. Mr. Mulligan said they were hiring. He wrote a short letter recommending me, and gave the letter to me.

Charlie, Petra, and Donald departed for their summer of exploring. They took the tent and one of the canoes. Charlie let me have the other canoe. I packed some things and left for Ely the same day. Ed Mulligan gave me a map that I managed to follow.

The route took me to Gunflint Lake. It's on the Canadian border and is a big, deep, impressive lake. It felt different from the lakes I had been on so far. Years later, I would learn that Gunflint Lake got its name from deposits of flint first discovered there by the Indians. It was originally called Flint Lake. The flint is located on some hills off the shoreline from Magnetic Bay. It comes from part of a comet that collided with Earth approximately 1.8 billion years ago. The biggest piece hit near Sudbury, Ontario. For hundreds of years, the Indians have used this unique metal and fought over who controlled it. The flint can be shaped into knives, spear points, and arrowheads. Later, it was discovered to work in flintlock rifles. Whoever controlled the flint was wealthy, because it was used or traded to other tribes and was even used as a source of currency. The Ojibwe have lived here, at a place called Flint Village, at least since the 1700s.

Over the centuries, other tribes tried to get possession of the flint. Ojibwe oral history tells of a great battle with the Sioux, who came to attack them. The Sioux were led by a chief named Black Dog from the Thunder Bay, Ontario, region. The Ojibwe knew they were going to be attacked, and called all their warriors within a hundred miles or more for help. The Sioux attacked. At first, the Sioux were winning and it looked bad for the Ojibwe. As the battle raged on, an Ojibwe medicine man called upon the Creator for help. The sky changed, and a terrible storm occurred. Heavy hail and terrible winds battered the Sioux. The tide of the battle changed; now the Ojibwe were winning. Many Sioux were killed. They were defeated and driven to the west, never to return in force in the region again.

On the Canadian side of the lake, I saw a train on some railroad tracks. There was a store and a small hotel along the tracks. I pulled in. The place was run by a trader and his Indian wife, whose names were George and Mary Plummer. I didn't know it then, but soon I'd be back. In future years, I would become good friends with the Plummers and their children, George, Walter, and Lillian.

The Plummers told me the train came from Port Arthur in Canada. It was called the PD&W Railway. That stood for Port Arthur, Duluth, and Western Railway. It had originally been built for an iron ore mine in the United States, called the Paulson Mine, located a couple of miles west of Gunflint. It was the same place to which Charlie Johnson had hauled supplies years earlier. The iron ore was very poor quality, and the mine went bust quickly. Only four or five trainloads of ore were ever hauled. The trestle over the Gunflint narrows burned, but the train still came from Port Arthur to Gunflint.

From here, I paddled down Magnetic Bay to the Granite River and followed it all the way to Saganaga Lake. Until I got close to Ely, I would continue to follow the international border.

I remembered Charlie's advice about needing to go down rapids bow heavy, and switched to the front seat when rapids appeared. Somehow, I managed to keep from getting dunked, and I made it to Saganaga. My canoe skills were getting better and I liked this method of travel.

Saganaga is a big lake with many islands, but there is also plenty of open water where the wind can blow. I was held up for most of a day getting around a place called American Point. The waves were white-capping and it was dangerous. I was learning to read the water and make decisions about when and how to go forward. Ed Mulligan's map showed only one cabin on the entire lake at this time. He said it was owned by Ed Connors and Mike Deschampes, a local Indian. I didn't try to find it.

Otter Track Lake is long and narrow. I got down it with no problems. Knife Lake is huge, with even more open expanses than Saganaga. The wind held me there for a day. Then it was on to Birch Lake, Basswood Lake, a four-mile portage to Fall Lake, and a town called Winton.

I sold the canoe, and now I was committed to staying. From Winton, I walked the four miles of road into Ely. I hadn't seen so many people since we came through Duluth. High grade iron ore had been discovered here in 1886. The Duluth and Iron Range Railways ran through town and led to at least two underground iron ore mines. I heard of many logging camps out in the woods. There were more than four thousand people in the two towns, with Winton being the larger. There were many government offices, and the whole area was bustling.

I asked around, and found the office of the International Boundary Commission. I went in and presented my letter. A nice young man asked me to wait. Pretty soon, another man came out and starting asking me questions. He wanted to know my name and age, where I had come from, how I got here, and what experience I had. He asked me questions about winter conditions and living in the woods. He must have liked my answers, because when we were done, he offered me a job.

I signed Alex Boostrom, my legal name, on the employment form. However, I told the man that everyone called me Alec, and that my dad's name was spelled Aleck. I said my dad chose Alex for me because he wanted it to look more American. This was more personal information than the poor guy needed to hear, but he smiled and listened patiently while I rattled on.

The Boundary Commission crews were working out on the lakes. The jobs involved running survey lines through the woods and down the lakes, both winter and summer. There were about fifty men in total. There were a few Canadians, but most were American.

There was one man from each country in charge. These two men's main job was to agree where the actual boundary would be located. Concrete monuments were built to mark the center of the border if it was on land. If it was on water, there were elaborate surveying offsets done, and we had to build monuments on shore to document them. If possible, these had to be ten feet in elevation above the high-water line.

The border followed the middle of most lakes. To get it accurately surveyed and permanently marked required both summer and winter work. You can't mix and pour cement in the winter. You can't accurately measure distances and angles down lakes in the summer. It was a big and complex operation. We worked on ahead with the winter surveying, and then came back with the summer work of building monuments. Our entire crew stayed pretty close together during both the summer and winter work.

I helped wash and screen sand and gravel wherever we could find it. When it was clean, we'd use it to mix with cement. The resulting concrete was first poured into a foundation dug in the ground. Then we'd pour a finer mixture of concrete into molds, three to four feet high, that were placed on top of the foundation in the exact position determined by the surveyors. Concrete in the mold was anchored into the foundation with steel rods.

An even better method was when we were over bedrock. Here, we would drill holes in the rock that were then used to pin and cement the monument in place. The top of the completed monument was marked with an official bronze cap with inscriptions.

I liked the work, and made myself as useful as possible. If something extra needed to be done, I would volunteer to do it. I was always cheerful and did my best to listen and learn. I was the first one ready to go in the morning, and tried to be the last one into the boats at the end of the day.

Whenever possible, the commission rented places for us to stay. They also hired local people to cook for us and help move us around. I met many folks I'd meet again in later years. I also got to know Winton and Ely pretty well from my time in the area.

At first I was called a gopher, which meant I'd go for or do anything I was asked to do. Over time, I came to realize I was good at two things: I was good with animals, and I had a mechanical ability to fix things. This was noticed by others. That first winter, I was assigned to help with the dog teams. The next summer, I was put with the boats, where I got to run the outboard motors and help the mechanic work on them.

We had the best of equipment. This included Woods Arctic sleeping bags filled with eiderdown, just like the one Ed Mulligan used. Our snowshoes were made by a company called Vermont Tubbs, and measured fourteen inches wide by forty-eight inches long. That company is still in business today, and their fourteen-by-forty-eight-inch model is what I still use when I can get them. One season is the most you can get out of the webbing, and after that they have to be relaced with long strips cut from moose hides. The frames, which are made from white ash, hold up pretty well.

Meanwhile, Petra and Charlie completed their summer of exploration. They decided to abandon their place at Moon Lake. After coming full circle, they knew they wanted to live on Clearwater, the lake at which Charlie had first camped when he originally came to Cook County. It's a beautiful, big, deep, lake trout lake, with high palisades rising over three hundred feet farther down on the south shore. A man named Lloyd Simmons owned 160 acres on the west end, with clear and legal title to the land. I think he got it via a homestead, but it could have been through a stone and timber claim, which could also provide for land ownership. He agreed to sell them eighty acres with a small cabin on it. In 1921, he sold them the other eighty acres.

Charlie and Petra got to work building another cabin immediately. I sent a letter that somehow reached them at Clearwater. They managed to get a letter back to me. We knew what each other was up to.

International Boundary Commission crew members.
COOK COUNTY HISTORICAL SOCIETY

Time seemed to fly. We methodically worked down the border country to Saganaga, and up the Granite River. We seemed to be getting more efficient, and we made good progress coming across the big lakes from Ely, but the Granite River took a very long time.

It wasn't all work, and on my days off I learned more about fishing. There is a saying about fishing lake trout that I have heard many times from my Indian friends. They know these fish are easiest to catch "when the popple buds are as big as a beaver's ear." This is during the spring, soon after the ice has gone out, when the trout can be found in the shallow water along the shorelines. I found this to be true. I had some great lake trout fishing, especially at Saganaga. In those days, there were no walleyes in the lake. They were introduced later, first by Art Nunsted, when he owned Chik Wauk Lodge, and then by the CCCs.

Over time, we all learned a lot about the history of the actual boundary line between Minnesota and Ontario. Our bosses shared many stories, and did a very good job educating us. They said the general location of the border had first been agreed to by the Treaty of Paris in 1783, at the conclusion of the Revolutionary War. It was agreed that the border would follow the usual water communication from Lake Superior to the northwest point on Lake of the Woods. The treaty language contained many vague details and some inaccurate information about the headwaters of the Mississippi River, which was thought to lie west of Lake of the Woods. By the early 1800s, this was found to be false. In 1842, Lord Ashburton, for the British, and Daniel Webster, representing the Americans, reached a formal agreement about the border location. They decided the international boundary should follow the "usual and customary route" of the voyageurs to the northwest point of Lake of the Woods, and that the voyageur portages along this route should be used in common by both countries. There was some question if that meant the Pigeon River route through

A completed boundary monument with one of the Boundary Commission surveyors.

Grand Portage, or the more northerly route starting at Ft. William. The Pigeon River route was the one agreed to in the 1842 Webster-Ashburton Treaty. Now, we were determining the exact location, and when we were done it would be nailed down precisely.

The two men in charge scrupulously followed the language in the two earlier treaties. However, when there were judgment calls to be made about a confusing segment, they usually decided in favor of Canada. Their reasoning was both sides believed the United States had gotten a better outcome near Lake of the Woods, and we had also received Isle Royale.

At some point, it was decided to move our headquarters from Ely to Cook County and locate it out in front of the operation. Grand Marais was selected, I guess, because it had good services and would not require another move until the project was completed in 1918.

As we got into the Gunflint Lake area, I was asked more and more questions about the land and the people up ahead. I recommended the Plummer's place on Gunflint Lake as a place to stay and get other help. The Plummers got some great business from us.

By now I knew Charlie had completed more cabins. He and Petra rented them to visitors, so I recommended their place on Clearwater as a base for our work camp when we arrived in that area. That turned out really well. Charlie did a lot of work for them. Petra was asked if she would cook for the entire crew. They told her the crew now numbered forty-seven men! She knew she could never handle this alone. Charlie sent word down to Milaca for his three sisters to come up to help. They agreed, and arrived quickly. Another girl from Grand Marais, whose name was Rose Zimmerman, was also hired. I didn't know it then, but I was destined to marry her sister.

We kept our eyes open, hoping to spot a white moose on Mountain Lake. The Indians at Gunflint had told us there was one around there, but we didn't see it. In later years, I don't think Charlie, or any of his children or guests, ever spotted one either.

Our progress slowed as we reached the smaller lakes because when the boundary was not over water, we had to cut the actual boundary line following the portages through the woods. They wanted the vegetation cut along the boundary at a minimum of twenty feet wide. The job was far from over, and I stayed with it till the end which, as planned, occurred during the fall of 1918.

Working for the Boundary Commission crew provided me with a variety of skills that were of benefit to me for the rest of my life. I learned to run a dog team and became good at repairing outboard motors. I had experience clearing line for surveyors and helping them measure distances with a steel chain. I intimately knew the border waters from Basswood Lake all the way down to the Pigeon River near Grand Portage. I knew most of the people along the route. I'd saved some money and was proud of what I'd done. Most important of all, I had grown up.

4

A Family of My Own

We received news of a terrible disaster in October, 1918. The Cloquet fire had killed more than 450 people. Many thousands more were seriously injured. The towns of Cloquet, Carlton, and Moose Lake were totally destroyed. Many smaller communities were also wiped out. Over 250,000 acres burned. These were the towns we had traveled through just four years earlier. We'd seen the people and their homes. This tragedy was very personal for me. It was, and still is, the worst forest fire in Minnesota history.

Thankfully, our parents' farm at Milaca was spared this time. Twenty-four years earlier, it had been completely destroyed by the Hinckley fire. They lost everything and had to rebuild. The Hinckley fire, in September of 1894, was almost as large as the Cloquet fire. It too, killed over four hundred people and burned at least two hundred thousand acres of forest. The town of Hinckley and other smaller towns nearby were destroyed. That fire also burned parts of Sandstone.

Everyone was stunned that something so terrible could happen again. If fires like that could happen down there, they could also happen up here. This realization resulted in the growth of both state and federal forestry operations in the following years. There was recognition, even then, that the forests needed to be managed, and people would need to be available to fight forest fires. Access was also deemed critical, and money for road-building increased.

The end of the border survey project in the fall of 1918 came at the same time I was required to register for the WWI draft. I had to go down to Milaca to register. They discovered I had flat feet and exempted me from serving in the military. My feet have always been a little strange, and it is not unusual at all for me to lose a couple of toenails after a particularly long day on snowshoes.

I returned to Clearwater to help Charlie and Petra. Charlie had not been idle. As soon as their first new log cabin was completed, he had built another. Then another. With each one, he became better and more efficient at turning them out in a high-quality manner.

Clearwater Lake acquired a reputation as a good place to catch lake trout. The deer population was increasing, and hunting was very good. People wanted to come here, and Charlie and Petra obliged. They were friendly and enjoyed renting and catering to visitors.

For the next three years, I kept very busy. I trapped mink in the fall and beaver in the spring. I ran the dog team I owned with Charlie and used it for winter trapping of marten and fisher. I guided hunters, fishermen, and canoeists, some to places like Ely; others I led north, deep into Canada. The standard pay for a guide in those days, and for many years to follow, was five dollars per day.

To carry food on these trips, I used cloth bags supplied by Petra. During her summers of canoe travel with Charlie she had used them to store flour, rice, raisins, sugar, beans, baking powder, and tea. Any food item needing storage went into them. They carry very well in a packsack and fit into any space. I still use cloth bags like this for my food today.

One winter, I moved down to East Bearskin Lake and trapped with a tough old-timer named Harry Hummitch. I'm not sure why he agreed to let me trap with him, but it might have had something to do with his age and being able to use the extra help. In addition to being a good log cabin builder, Harry was a very good trapper. I learned a lot from him. The following winter we trapped together again.

The first winter we worked from his main cabin on East Bearskin over to his trapping cabin located in a hidden spot near the east end of Crocodile Lake. From here, one of our traplines went up into the vegetable chain of lakes toward Greenwood Lake. Another continued up the Crocodile River to near Stump Lake. Harry's old cabin is still there on Crocodile River. I put a new roof on it and did other repairs to the place a number of years ago when I trapped mink out of it. It's still in good condition.

That second year we gave the area surrounding the Crocodile River and the vegetable chain of lakes a rest. Our main trapline went west over to Poplar Lake, to Meads Lake and the other Moon Lake, then to Finn Lake and down the long creek to the east end of Long Island Lake where we had a wall tent and stove. I really liked it there. I didn't know it then, but I would develop a lifelong attraction to Long Island Lake.

Harry taught me how to properly maintain steel traps and snares. Left untreated, they rust. Rusty traps make a mess in your packsack, and can eventually become damaged or fail to spring shut properly. The way to stop the rust is to dye your traps black. The dye is made with water and many strips of green alder bark (sumac can also be used). Let it soak for days or even weeks in a tub or barrel. When the water turns black, put your traps right in with the bark. Stir the whole works every day or two. When one batch of traps is done, put in the next. If you have a steel tub or barrel, an even better method is to heat it to boiling and soak your traps in the alder bark mixture. They come out a rich black that will remain on them for years.

Harry showed me a technique he uses in the spring to add to his food supply. I've had some success with it in years since. When open water appears and the ducks start nesting, carry a soft lead pencil. When you come upon a duck nest, mark an X on each egg. When you pass by a day or two later, gather the eggs without an X. They are guaranteed fresh as they have had little time to develop under their mother.

Another new food Harry introduced me to is beaver liver. They are small, about the size of a fifty-cent piece. You fry them and place them on top of pancakes. Harry said this is the way all the old-timers did it. I am still doing it, too.

Harry also ate a lot of rabbits during the winter, and he showed me how to snare and fix them for supper.

We always stopped for lunch each day. We'd build a fire and put water or snow into the teapot we always carried. Once the water started to get warm, we'd put a small amount of bulk tea into a little aluminum ball-like container that hung on a chain inside the pot. We'd let the water boil for a couple of minutes and it turned to a strong, good-tasting tea. We'd drink it with sugar and it was a high-energy drink that gave us a good lift. If we didn't have store-bought tea, we'd use Labrador tea Harry had found in the swamps during the fall.

For food at lunch, it was always two pancakes left over from breakfast. If we had some meat we would wrap it inside. If we had no meat, we just ate the pancakes while we drank our tea. This is still how I have lunch when I am trapping out in the woods.

We all smoked and chewed tobacco, but Harry also got me chewing spruce gum. He'd pick a hard lump of clear pitch that had formed from a wound on a white spruce tree and pop it in his mouth. I still chew it occasionally.

Harry was famous for going around in the winter without a hat. He had a good head of hair, and somehow it kept his head and ears warm. Everyone talked about this and wanted to be just like Harry. I tried, but couldn't get away with it. A WWI vet named Benny Ambrose had come to Grand Portage around 1919 or 1920 with a fellow returning soldier. After a short time, he moved to our area. Soon Benny was seen going around without a hat, and he bragged to people that he was just as tough as Harry Hummitch. However, someone saw him a while later and his ears were sort of shriveled and black. Benny wore a hat after that.

Harry built a number of other log cabins at East Bearskin. His place went on to become the lodge with the same name. He also trapped along the North Shore above Hovland for a couple of winters.

The local newspaper ran a sort of gossip column, and always tried to report which trappers had come into town to sell fur and where they had come from. You could never tell where trappers had been by talking with them. We trappers were notorious for giving false information.

One winter I needed to run the dog team from Clearwater down to Grand Marais for supplies. It turned out to be a fine winter day

Benny Ambrose at a trapping cabin. Cook County Historical Society

and I was up long before daylight. My dogs loved to run at night and much preferred that time for travel. I guess there are more animals out moving around during those hours and it's in the dogs' blood to do the same.

I harnessed the team and off we went. Conditions were perfect. The trail was well-broken and the snow was firm. The dogs wanted to run, and I just let them go. We came off the twisting, hilly side trail leading to Clearwater and turned down what later came to be called the Gunflint Trail. We were really moving.

We went past Swamper Cariboo's place at the 22 Mile Post. This was on the north side of Swamper Lake that's named after him. His dogs barked, but we never even slowed down.

Five miles later, down at the 17 Mile Post, we were still going strong. The creek at that location used to be called 17 Mile Creek, but in recent years someone changed its name to Lullaby Creek.

I called a halt at the 15 Mile Post by the old South Brule River bridge and gave the dogs a rest for the steep climb ahead. They weren't quite as frisky as they had been earlier. In those days, what became the "old" Gunflint Trail ran right up over Pine Mountain, which is at the 13 Mile Post, then down through Maple Hill and straight down the hill into Grand Marais. In a few years a new route would be completed, which would cross the South Brule a few miles farther downstream. The "new" Gunflint Trail goes east around Pine Mountain. It's three miles longer with a much gentler grade.

We made it in three hours and twenty minutes. That is my all-time record for the thirty-two-mile trip. I tied the team down outside the Paine Hotel and went inside for breakfast. An attractive part-Indian girl asked what I wanted to eat. I ordered pancakes, of course. However, I was more interested in her. She served me pancakes and coffee. I didn't want to leave, and stayed for several coffee refills.

I learned her name was Josephine Zimmerman and that people called her Jo. She is half-Indian, and her dad was janitor at the county courthouse. I told her I knew her sister Rose. I spent the night at the Paine Hotel and took her out for supper. I returned several more times that winter, courting Jo and getting to know her parents. By spring, we were engaged.

Jo's parents were both very unique. Her dad, Sam, was a survivor of the Sioux Indian revolt in western Minnesota, Iowa, and the Dakota Territory. It is called the Dakota War of 1862. Sam's father and two brothers were killed near New Ulm. Ten-year-old Sam, his mother, and two sisters survived. His parents had put a dress on Sam, and the group of Sioux they encountered spared the women and girls. More than six thousand Sioux made war on the settlers in western Minnesota, northwestern Iowa, and eastern Dakota Territory for over a month. Hundreds of white people were killed, and many women and girls were taken captive and horribly abused. Thousands of acres of crops were destroyed.

The cause of the fighting was the failure of Congress to provide annuity payments promised to the Sioux in their 1858 treaty. Congress was preoccupied with the Civil War. The winter of 1862 was very bad, and the Sioux had little to eat. Cutworms had ruined what corn they had planted the year before. The annuity payments of fifteen dollars per person were promised to arrive in June of each year. Already, by June, some of the Indians had starved to death.

By August, the situation was even more extreme. The payments had not yet arrived, and store owners refused to provide many of the Sioux more credit to buy food. These store owners had always provided credit previously, and many times an individual Indian's entire allotment was owed to a store. This time, many more of the Indians were on the verge of starvation. It all came to a head when a delegation of Sioux went to the Indian Agency, demanding food and pointing out that the store owners' shops were full. One of the store owners told the Indians they could eat grass as far as he was concerned. It took only couple of days for this story to quickly spread among the Indians. Meanwhile, there was an incident involving four very hungry Indian boys who found some eggs in the woods, which had been laid by a white woman's hens. She tried to get them back, and was killed. This, along with the comment about eating grass, was what blew the lid off and the revolt was on. The store owner was one of the first casualties found. His mouth had been stuffed with grass.

In response, Colonel Sibley led a force that defeated the Sioux and rescued many of the captives. His forces captured many of the Sioux responsible and drove the others who had revolted out of Minnesota, Iowa, and eastern Dakota. Some of the Sioux who escaped would go on to help defeat General Custer fourteen years later in Montana. Others who had not revolted were taken out of the region. They came back, continued to farm, and were peaceful. They're still there today.

A military commission tried 425 of the Indians captured by Col. Sibley and sentenced 303 of them to death. President Lincoln commuted most of the sentences, and thirty-eight were hanged. Sam's mother had to go to St. Paul to attend the commission hearings and help identify the Indians who killed her husband and sons. She, Sam, and her two daughters were brought to Mankato to witness the hangings. Over four thousand people were there to watch.

One day after the outbreak, the annuity money from Washington arrived at the Indian Agency. It was seventy-one thousand dollars in gold coins. The whole terrible tragedy might have been avoided if the money had arrived one day sooner. The final delay that held it up was due to government indecision over whether to make the payments in gold or paper money.

Two years later, Sam's mother died. Sam and his sister, Elizabeth, were sent to Duluth to live with an uncle. Elizabeth soon married Jacob Hangartner from Beaver Bay. Sam lived with them until he was fourteen when he moved out to work on his own. He worked at a number of jobs, including driving oxen in lumber camps and as a cook on a boat on Lake Superior. Next, he went to work for Henry Mayhew in Duluth. In 1874, Cook County was created by the Minnesota legislature. That same year, the Mayhews sent twenty-two-year-old Sam to Grand Marais to work for both Thomas and Henry Mayhew at their trading post. Sam also became a trapper and commercial fisherman.

As a child, Sam had burned both his legs. During the winter of 1887, he froze both his legs and feet while on his trapline. It was in the area of the old burns. He managed to get back to Grand Marais, but no one there could treat him. Fortunately, there was still a boat running to Duluth, and they put him on it. Sam returned, having had his right leg amputated above the knee. He never let that slow him down.

Sam did more and more trapping in the winter and commercial fishing in the summer. He always used just one crutch. In the winter, he strapped a regular snowshoe on his good left foot. He attached a modified snowshoe to his right peg leg. A smaller platform was attached to his crutch. Legend has it Indians saw his strange tracks and called the nearby lake "Devil Track." Sam never denied the story, although there are some who say the lake received its name before this event. I prefer to believe it was Sam's tracks that inspired the unique name.

For commercial fishing, Sam got paid one dollar per hundred-pound barrel of salted lake trout. I don't know what he got for herring or whitefish, but it had to be less. For the one dollar lake trout price, he also had to provide the salt and barrel. Henry Mayhew set up a business out on the Point to make barrels. He had brought up a barrel cooper named George Falconer. Falconer and his crew split wood and shaved it by hand. They could turn out an average of six kegs per man per day. I never heard Sam say if he was ever able to get his kegs returned so he could reuse them or if he always had to buy new ones. It must have been a tough business.

Sam would row his fishing boat along the lakeshore. One day he stopped at the Indian village called Chippewa City, located just east of Grand Marais. Approximately two hundred people lived there. A pretty Indian girl was picking berries down by the shore. She didn't know English, and Sam couldn't speak her language, but they managed to communicate. Her name was Jane Maymaushkowaush Elliot. Soon they married. She was Jo's mother.

Sam built a home twenty-five miles farther up the shore at Cannonball Bay, located just inside the Grand Portage Reservation boundary. He raised his nine children there until his son, Willie, was killed by a kick in the head from a horse. Sam's wife Jane refused to go back in the house or let her family live there for another day. This was a common belief with the Indians. When someone was killed at their home, they immediately moved out. Jane started walking away and her family followed.

The family carried their belongings, and started the long walk on the shoreline trail to Grand Marais. By the first night they had made it to what is now called the Kadunce River, where they stayed with two Indians named Paul and Joe Kadunce. The next day they made it to Chippewa City. They lived there for some time before eventually moving to Grand Marais.

After the county courthouse was constructed, Sam became the janitor. For eighteen years, he shoveled coal into the boiler, cut the grass on the big lawn outside, and kept the inside of the building clean and tidy. All on one leg.

Jane Maymaushkowaush Elliot had relatives up and down the North Shore. Hers is a very well-known Indian name and it would open many doors for me with the Indians in the years that followed.

Alec Boostrom wedding portrait.
BOOSTROM FAMILY PHOTO

Jo Zimmerman.
BOOSTROM FAMILY PHOTO

Much earlier, there was a Chief Maymaushkowash who was a relation. Jane was very knowledgeable about many things, from preparing game and fish, to serving as a midwife, to Ojibway culture and traditions.

Jo and I married the summer of 1921. I dressed in the finest clothes I could buy, and even had a portrait taken. Except for working for the US Geological Survey a few years later, and trapping for two winters with Charlie, this marked the end of my work at Clearwater.

I bought a house in Grand Marais down by the west side of the harbor. Betty was born at home in 1922. Jo's mother, Jane, was the midwife. In 1925 our second daughter, Jean, was also born at home. Again, Jane was the midwife. Jo had complications with Jean's birth. They were both okay, but that was the end of any more children for us. I was now a father, and I had more responsibilities.

Jean quickly acquired the nickname, "Sister." She never lost it, and that is still how everyone in the family refers to her.

More people were arriving to the region and I was always able to find work. I bought a Model T Ford and quickly learned how to drive and repair it. One of my jobs during that time was as a mechanic for Homer Massie at his Ford garage.

One winter day, Ole Anderson came in, towing his new car with a horse. I looked it over and quickly determined the problem.

"Ole, your engine block is cracked," I told him. "Have you been using antifreeze in the radiator?"

"Antifreeze? I've been using my special spring water. I've seen that spring flowing at forty below and it has never frozen."

What could I say to logic like that? Ole was a proud old guy and I had to be gentle in explaining how water flowing from deep underground comes to the surface at a temperature above freezing. Maybe we were part of the problem with briefing new car owners. Homer came out from his office to talk with Ole. From then on, he made doubly certain new car buyers understood the importance of both anti-freeze and oil.

The Alger-Smith Railway was coming. By 1916 it had already reached Cascade Lake, where construction farther eastward had stopped. Logging camps were located all over the west end of the county. We were sure a spur line would be built to Grand Marais. A route had even been located that ended near my house down by the harbor. We were very disappointed when the line was not built. For the next ten years or so, there was no further railroad construction to the east.

I saw Ed Mulligan from time to time. He was working as a federal forest ranger. After a while, he was no longer cruising timber or surveying. He had aged a lot. One year, he was no longer with us.

I became a game warden/trapper for a short time, but that didn't work out. The duties included law enforcement and trapping predators. I'll tell you more about it later. For a while, I rented a small building and hung out my shingle as a repairman for cars and outboard motors. Business was never good, and I had to give it up. I realized I missed trapping and being out in the woods. I liked the independence of that lifestyle too, but now I had a family to support.

Time moved along, and the girls were growing. Construction of the Alger-Smith Railway started moving eastward again. It was built to Two Island Lake, and came by Frank Hopkins's place. Frank was a local trapper. The railroad turned northeast and went up and crossed Pine Lake. A long, wooden trestle was constructed there, just like the shorter one built years earlier across the narrows at Gunflint Lake. From Pine Lake, the railroad goes north between East and West Twin Lakes and then on up the flat country toward the east side of Lima Mountain. Numerous spurs were constructed off to the sides.

Somewhere along there, the ownership of the private timber changed to the Weyerhaeuser Company. They had acquired rights to both the private land and the timber by buying up and consolidating all the old stone and timber claims that had been filed. That program had been shut down prior to creation of the national forest. Those stone and timber claims must have been lucrative for people. As I understand it, you could file for up to 160 acres and receive clear title to both the land and the timber. You did not have to build a residence on the land, but it wasn't completely free. There was a minimum payment of at least $2.50 per acre if the government did not complete an appraisal of both the land and the timber within nine months of the application. I'm not sure how many appraisals were ever done. The national forest people must have also sold timber rights to the companies in order for them to log an area economically.

Construction of the railroad really moved ahead. The line continued north, all the way up past the northwest end of Clearwater, down along Daniels Lake, and finally to Rose Lake at the border. The stock market crash of 1929 brought everything to a halt. Rails were never even laid for the last five miles down to Rose Lake.

The Weyerhaeuser Company soon gave title to their land and timber to the Superior National Forest. I suppose this was done to avoid the county taxes. The great distance lumber would have to be hauled to markets was probably another factor. It was not unusual for the national forest to receive big additions like this from many of the other timber companies. What was different about this situation was Weyerhaeuser never even logged most of their land around the Gunflint Trail region. Expansion of the national forest was not all from free donations from the timber companies. The Weeks Act of 1911 set up a government program to purchase some of these big land holdings. Today, the Superior National Forest has increased in size from its initial 1.2 million acres to over three million acres because of additions like this.

In the 1920s, huge sums of Federal money became available for the building of new roads. A new road was proposed between Ely and the Gunflint Trail, but the proposal was quickly killed by someone from Washington, named Jardine, who was Secretary of Agriculture over the Forest Service. I'm glad that never happened. However, many other roads were built.

The Fernberg Road east of Ely was completed to Snowbank Lake and Lake One, which is on the North Kawishiwi River. A side road was built up to Moose Lake. Now, the access both to Knife Lake and to Lake Insula became shorter and easier. Kawishiwi Lodge was built soon after the road got out to Lake One. In another ten years, a fire lookout tower would be built near the end of the road and a major trail would be constructed across the Superior Primitive Area to the Gunflint Trail.

A new road was proposed between Ely and Buyck. It was built, and is called the Echo Trail.

The road near Clearwater was extended to Gunflint Lake, and soon came to be called the Gunflint Trail. Gunflint Lodge was built. Other resorts on other lakes were also constructed. Balsam Grove Lodge on Poplar Lake and Swanson's Lodge on Hungry Jack Lake are just two of them. Later, the Gunflint Trail was extended to Seagull and then Saganaga. A side road off the Gunflint Trail was completed to Clearwater.

Charlie and Petra decided to build a massive lodge. Charlie hired help, and they started in 1925. It took two years to complete. It is a huge forty-by-sixty-foot pine log building with two stories and fourteen rooms upstairs. Charlie built the diamond willow furniture over two more winters. Clearwater Lodge is beautiful, and became very well-known. Charlie and Petra raised their ten children there.

The lower sixteen miles of the Gunflint Trail was relocated, and a new road was built. The new road starts in Grand Marais and angles up the steep Sawtooth Ridge above town. It has a much gentler grade compared to the old road that ran mostly straight down the hill. The new road continues on through eastern Maple Hill and crosses the Devil Track River near Andrew Hedstrom's sawmill. From here, the road runs up through the stand of old growth white pine, and ties into the old Gunflint Trail near the old 16 Mile Post.

During this time, there was a proposal to build a massive series of dams along the border country. A timber industry man named Backus, along with a number of other influential Canadian and American partners, wanted a series of dams that would flood the country from North Lake all the way west to Rainy Lake near International Falls. They wanted to log along this vast corridor, using the huge lakes that would be created. They also intended to generate power from the dams. Both countries contributed money to fund studies.

From 1925 until 1929, there were US Army Corps of Engineers survey crews and aerial photography planes running lake and stream studies all along both sides of the border. The headquarters was in Duluth and from there, military pilots flew the aerial photo flights. They had some big camps on Northern Light and Saganaga Lakes.

Joe Russel's store in Winton provided most of the supplies for the main project. Dusty Rhoades, a pilot from Vermillion Lake, flew a lot of the stuff out to the camps. Charlie Johnson's store in Grand Marais also did a good business with them.

The US Geological Survey was involved. For a while, they worked out of Clearwater Lodge. I got a job with them, based on my prior experience on the boundary survey. A young surveyor named Wesson Cook was in charge. He worked for the US Geological Survey in Washington, D.C. Wes befriended me even though we had little in common at first. We had no idea where our friendship would lead.

Soon, it was announced that Wes Cook was engaged to Rose Zimmerman, my sister-in-law, who was still working for Petra and Charlie at Clearwater. They decided to wait to be married until

Wes's job was completed, and the event could take place at his home back in Maryland. We were happy for them. Wes and I became even closer friends.

Rose Lake on the international border is named for Rose Zimmerman. Wes's position with the US Geological Survey allowed him to assign official names to some of the lakes.

Many locals, including my good friend Art Smith, worked for the US Army Corps of Engineers out in their camps. Art told me he couldn't believe the amount of salt pork they were served. The Army had seemingly endless surplus quantities of it in big tin cans, left over from WWI, and they were determined to use it up.

After all the work and money spent on the studies and planning by both the Americans and Canadians, there was very little public support for this massive undertaking. Ernest Oberholtzer, from Mallard Island on Rainy Lake, spoke eloquently against it and organized some very effective opposition. A group called the Izaak Walton League did the same. They even had local chapters in Grand Marais and Ely. Most everyone I knew was also against it. It took until 1930 before Congress finally killed it for good by passing a law called the Shipstead-Newton-Nolan Act.

Something remains today from this project that is worth mentioning. The outlet of Saganaga was where one of the big dams was proposed. At the outlet in Cache Bay, the river goes over Silver Falls and then north to Saganagons. You either pull into the portage on the right, or you go over the falls. Lives have been lost in the strong undertow in the huge pool below the falls. Today, there is a heavy steel cable strung across the river just before the falls. Most visitors think this is some kind of last ditch safety net for people in boats or canoes who could grab it to keep from being swept over the falls. It might work for that now, but in reality, the cable was put there to support a cable car used by the stream survey guys for taking current measurements. Someone must have decided to lower the cable and leave it there for the sake of safety.

We still lived in our house down by the harbor in Grand Marais. We had yet to acquire electricity, and one of the girls' jobs was pumping up the Coleman lantern each night for our light. They still remember pumping exactly fifty strokes. When the pressure ran down, the light was out for the night.

I continued to work at various jobs. I kept up with news from up the Gunflint Trail and along the rest of border country as best I could. That country was in my blood. Working in town wasn't helping to get me back to the land I had come to love.

5

The Game Wardens

In 1909, the same year the 1.2 million-acre Superior National Forest was created, the Minnesota legislature decided that all of it should be managed as a game refuge. There is a clear separation of power between the state and the feds. The US Forest Service manages the national forest lands. The State of Minnesota manages the fish and wildlife on them. If the state wanted a huge game refuge, they got to have a huge game refuge, whether it made sense or not.

As the national forest expanded, so did the boundaries of the game refuge. The northern parts of Cook, Lake, and St. Louis counties were all included. It was a massive area, and it directly affected many people's lives.

Enforcement of refuge regulations up here was sporadic for many years. The refuge was too big to be effectively managed. The location of public land, where the refuge rules applied, and the location of private land, where they didn't, was confusing. Conflicting stone and timber claims, along with settlers who believed they had legitimately homesteaded, were a big part of the problem. Good maps were another. Most of us knew little or nothing about any of this. However, it was all part of what Ed Mulligan had talked about with us years earlier.

The Minnesota Department of Natural Resource's Game and Fish Division finally got serious about enforcing their game refuge regulations. They had a publicity campaign with newspaper stories. Their message was that animals, particularly moose, but also deer and beaver, needed a massive wilderness sanctuary where they would be free to disperse throughout the rest of the state.

The state also wanted something called predator control to occur in the game refuge. Trapping and snaring of wolves, fox and lynx had always been going on, but now the department wanted a much more concentrated effort from its own people.

This made no sense to us. The whole concept was flawed thinking, and we experienced trappers knew it. Animals don't behave this way. The condition of their habitat is very important for healthy populations, and it was in pretty good shape throughout the state. Also, as far as we knew, their populations were not in serious trouble elsewhere. To think that a complete prohibition on any harvesting of beaver over a million or more acres, was necessary to protect these animals was completely wrong.

Metal game refuge signs were put up throughout the national forest. They were identical to the ones you see today between the highway and the shoreline of Lake Superior. Fisher and marten got added to the list of protected species in the massive refuge. Many new wardens were hired and cabins were built for them out in the Superior Primitive Area. Incidentally, over the years this area was also called the Superior Wilderness Area; sometimes it was called the Superior Roadless Area; and sometimes the Quetico-Superior Area. None of us could ever keep the official name straight.

My brother, Charlie, was the first of us to be hired as a game warden/trapper by the state. These could be part-time jobs, and that's the way he worked for them. In 1923, he arrested Joe Chosa and another guy with twenty-four beaver during late November. The Chosas are a well-known Indian family throughout the border region, especially around Ely. At this time, Henry Chosa was running the Four-Mile Portage from Fall Lake to Basswood using a Model T Ford truck. Leo Chosa ran the trading post on Basswood, and had a gasoline fishing boat. The Chosas originally came up here from the Lac du Flambeau Reservation in Wisconsin. They still have relatives there.

The next year, game warden George Mayhew arrested Swamper Cariboo and Leo Zimmerman, my brother-in-law, at Tucker Lake for trapping beaver. I don't remember how many they were caught with.

George Mayhew is said to be the first white child born in Cook County. Based on stories told to me by my Indian mother-in-law,

Jane Zimmerman, I'm not so sure of that. There were white people coming and going, and living at Grand Portage for a hundred or more years earlier. One story tells of a boy born to the Elliot family in Grand Portage around the 1830s. Another story tells of a trading post at Grand Marais in the 1820s and '30s. It was run by a white family who supposedly also had a child.

Regardless of whether or not he was the first white child born in the county, George was a good man. He was fired from the game warden job for some offensive remark he made that was overheard by one of their roaming investigators. These investigators were political appointees with no law enforcement experience. I felt sorry for George. On top of his employment troubles, his wife was very sickly. George went to work for the Army Corps of Engineers, surveying the lakes in the border country for the series of dams that were being proposed. After two years with them, he was hired back as a game warden. His wife died a year later. George worked as a game warden for a number of years.

Based on my observations and stories I heard, it was not unusual for game wardens to be fired by one of the roaming political appointees who seemed to spy on the field game wardens. The Division of Game and Fish had some terrible problems with cronyism and low morale in those days. Fortunately, there were some excellent field game wardens, and eventually the division was cleaned up and put under the state civil service. The other divisions in the Department of Natural Resources, such as forestry, did not seem to have these troubles based on stories told to me by my friend Patty Bayle, the local state forest ranger.

Frank Hopkins lived at his cabin on Two Island Lake. In the winter of 1925, game warden Joe Brickner was on patrol, and came upon Hopkins, who was drunker than a skunk on some moonshine. This was during Prohibition. Brickner didn't want to get involved with this petty offense, but since it was cold and Hopkins was so drunk, Brickner built a fire, made a pot of strong black coffee, and stayed with him until he sobered up. While talking his head off, Hopkins told Brickner to tell game warden Charlie Ott to "keep

Game Warden Charlie Ott with two timber wolves. COOK COUNTY HISTORICAL SOCIETY

away from me in the woods, or he won't come out alive." Of course, as soon as he got back to town, Brickner relayed this threat to Charlie. Charlie didn't seem very concerned and said, "If I have a reason to bring Frank Hopkins in, I will bring him in."

That spring, warden Brickner again came upon Frank Hopkins, who was walking down the Gunflint Trail. This time Frank had a packsack full of fresh beaver hides. Hopkins gave him no trouble. He admitted the beaver were his and pled guilty. His sentence was a fine or three months in jail. He chose the jail time. Afterward, he told people it was a good summer. He didn't have to find work, they let him out of jail every day to work on public facilities around town, and they fed him three good meals each day.

There was no more news about Frank Hopkins for some time. About ten days after Christmas, Brickner ran into a trapper named Ray Robinson in Grand Marais. Robinson lived over by Cascade Lake, near the end of the Alger-Smith Railway line, about ten miles west of Hopkins' cabin on Two Island Lake. Robinson said he'd spent Thanksgiving with Hopkins and Frank was supposed to come to his place for Christmas. He hadn't shown up. Brickner told Charlie Ott. The more they talked, the more the two of them became worried.

Charlie harnessed his dog team and started on the eighteen-mile trip to Two Island Lake. The snow was deep and soft. It took him two days to reach the place, because he had to break trail on snowshoes ahead of the team. Charlie would tie the sled to a tree, with the team attached, snowshoe out ahead in the deep snow, turn around, and snowshoe back. He'd take off his snowshoes, put them in the sled, and drive the team over the broken trail. Then he'd repeat the process, again and again.

When Charlie finally got to the cabin, he found Frank in bed with both feet badly frozen, and gangrene about to set in. Both his feet were horribly discolored, and it looked like they would have to be amputated. Charlie put Frank in his sleeping bag and wrapped other blankets around him. He tied Frank in his dogsled and mushed non-stop back to Grand Marais on the now packed and frozen trail. Dr. Hicks was able to save both of Frank's feet, and only had to cut one toe off each of them.

Charlie had the last word. He said to Brickner, "I told you I would bring Frank Hopkins in if I had a reason to."

In 1926, game warden/trapper Carl Sjoberg, from Grand Marais, was patrolling the Good Harbor Hill area west of town with Archie Klawon, a warden from Wheaton who was temporarily assigned to help at Grand Marais. They came upon a local guy who had shot a deer. This was a clear case of poaching. The man's rifle was leaning against a nearby tree, and he was skinning the deer. Carl Sjoberg tried to sneak up quietly, but the guy spotted him. He grabbed his rifle, pointed it at Sjoberg, and hollered for him not to come any closer. Klawon was an excellent shot. Although he was fifty yards away, he drew his pistol, fired once from the hip and nailed the guy in the leg. The poacher was knocked down and his rifle went flying.

Sjoberg and Klawon brought the wounded guy to Dr. Hicks in Grand Marais. After removing four layers of clothing, they discovered the wound was superficial, and the bullet was found loose in the guy's pant leg. People around town said Klawon had deliberately aimed for his leg, and could have killed him if he wanted to. The two wardens charged him with taking a deer out of season, resisting arrest, and assault with a deadly weapon. The county attorney refused to prosecute. He told the wardens the wound was punishment enough. This was a good example of the lack of support for the game laws because of the fact that people needed the meat to feed their families. It would happen again and again.

That same year, I applied for a job as game warden/trapper and was hired. The pay was one hundred dollars a month. A field game warden was paid $125 a month. I wasn't committed to the mission, and didn't believe it made any sense, but I needed the work. I applied for the job because it meant I got to be back out in the woods. They gave me some basic training, and issued me a badge. One of their rules was we should always try to work in pairs. This made sense for law enforcement work, and I always tried to follow it.

I fit in, and my supervisor, Joe Brickner, seemed to like me. Another game warden named Art Johnson and I were selected to help with a big VIP trip to Brule Lake, which is twenty-five miles northwest of Grand Marais. There were over three dozen newspaper people, politicians, high-ranking state DNR officials, and others in the group. It was during the winter, and we traveled by snowshoe and dog team. Half of the group came from Ely, which is sixty miles to the west, and the other half came from Grand Marais. Once we joined at Brule Lake, we stayed in an Alger-Smith logging camp that was not being used. There were several days of long discussions that went far into the night. The highlight for me was to meet and spend time with some of the best of the old-time game wardens in the state. I got to meet Jack Linklater and Bill Hanson from Winton, and also Archie Klawon, who was working out of the St. Paul headquarters.

My first big case occurred just outside of Grand Marais. I got a tip that Benny Ambrose and two of his friends would be coming down the Gunflint Trail with a load of illegal beaver hides. The word was they planned to sneak them into town that night. I notified Brickner, my supervisor, and he directed two of us to set up a road-block where the road narrows at a place called "The Pines." Joe came along to oversee the operation.

Sure enough, later that night, a truck appeared. When its occupants saw our roadblock up ahead, they stopped and threw some packs into the woods. They took off on foot into the woods, but not before I identified all three. We retrieved the packs, and discovered two of them contained a total of fifty-five beaver hides, which we confiscated. The third pack contained clothes, toilet articles and an undeveloped roll of film. When it was developed, it showed two of the guys holding captive bear cubs. This was also illegal.

When we had our case prepared, we charged Benny and his two friends for illegal possession of beaver. They pled not guilty, and hired an experienced lawyer from Ely. He demanded a jury trial, which was held in Grand Marais. We three game wardens all testified what we had seen, and the fact we had identified the three men with their beaver at the Pines on that particular evening. We also present-ed the developed film as evidence. For the defense, a local guy named Herb Valentine testified under oath that all three of them had been at his cabin on Loon Lake both for supper that night and breakfast the next morning. Loon Lake is located just before Gunflint Lake and is another thirty miles or so farther up the Gunflint Trail. Our prosecuting attorney never even asked Valentine if he had seen them there between supper and breakfast.

When the jury heard Valentine, their minds were made up. They found all three defendants not guilty. The defendants were free to go, but the state got to keep the illegal beaver, which were later sold at auction for about $1500, approximately $30 apiece. The defendants also had the nerve to ask for the third packsack full of personal gear to be returned to them, even though they denied it was theirs during the trial. They got it.

This left a terrible taste in my mouth. I didn't like the confronta-tion. I was sympathetic to the trappers, as the jurors obviously were. I didn't believe in the game refuge. Another game warden who was not even directly involved became so disgusted he quit.

I needed the money, so I stayed with it. I requested to work far out in the Primitive Area, and got my wish. They assigned another warden and me to work out of the new cabin located on an island in the southwest end in the Little Saganaga area. It had been built only a year earlier. Our job was law enforcement patrol and trapping predators. This was more to my liking.

By now it was 1927. During the late winter, Ray, my partner, could no longer take the solitude and primitive living conditions. We hadn't seen a soul. I really enjoyed living out there, but Ray told me he planned to quit. We snowshoed to town and reported in. Ray's leaving created a big problem for Joe Brickner. There was no one available to immediately send back with me, so I volunteered my brother, Charlie, who was also trained as a game warden/trapper. He had completed construction of Clearwater Lodge one year earlier, and I figured he would be able to make at least one trip and could use the extra money.

Brickner contacted Charlie, and he agreed. We left a couple of days later for Little Sag. There still didn't appear to be anyone around. We set traps and snares for wolves and fox. In spite of knowing it was illegal, we set some traps for beaver. We caught some, and brought their hides out with us when our trip ended.

We sold them and more than doubled our monthly salary. Word soon reached Joe Brickner, who ordered us in and questioned us. We knew he had no evidence and could never prove it, but Charlie and I weren't going to lie. We admitted what we had done. Joe fired both of us on the spot. I'm ashamed and embarrassed about this event in my life, and wish I had it to do over again. Not because I broke the game laws—I would have to do plenty more of that—but because I accepted the state's money and violated their trust in me. Out West, I think it's called "riding for the brand."

Over the years, the game refuge rules were gradually relaxed. The one prohibiting deer hunting went first. But the prohibition on trapping beaver and fisher in the Primitive Area remained for several more decades, and caused many of us to have to break the law to make a living and feed our families.

One year, game wardens Johnny Blackwell and Art Johnson returned to Grand Marais after a three-week-long trip. They had covered a huge amount of country on snowshoes, beginning at Sawbill Lake and ending at Gunflint Lake. They'd been as far west as the state cabin on Insula and the Forest Service cabin on Kekekabic. When they got back to town, they went to the state warehouse first. They turned in their equipment and the predator hides they had trapped to the man in charge. With this accomplished, they went to the office to write their reports and read their mail. They discovered they had been laid off for two of the previous three weeks! Johnny now wishes they would have gone to the office first. That way they could have at least turned in the predators for the $22.50 bounty payment each and sold their hides. His wife, Selma, cried and cried over this loss of her husband's salary. Blackwell quit the state shortly after this episode. Art Johnson is still with them today.

One year Charlie Ott came upon H.P. Lyght, who had just killed a deer out of season. Charlie had no choice but to arrest him and confiscate the deer. H.P. was a Negro man who came with his wife to the Lutsen area in the late 1920s. They purchased a place on the Caribou Trail and raised their family. They are the only black people in our county.

Like everyone else during the Depression, they scraped to get by. Most people called H.P. "Hosie Posie." He had a big garden, and during the summer he sold his produce in Lutsen and Grand Marais. H.P. and his wife had six kids; four big strong boys and two girls. All four boys went on to become loggers.

H.P. said he would plead guilty. His sentencing date came, and he appeared in Grand Marais before the local judge. H.P. was sworn in.

The first question from the judge was, "H.P., did you kill that deer?"

"Yes sir, your honor, sir, I did."

Next it was, "Have you ever done that before?"

"Yes sir, your honor, sir, I have."

"About how many times would you say you have done it before?"

H.P. needed some time to answer this one. Finally, he said, "Your honor, sir, it takes a deer a week to feed my family."

The judge never hesitated. He slammed down his gavel and said, "Case dismissed!"

H.P. and his wife have passed on, but some of their children still remain in the county. I'm proud to report their youngest son, John, is our current sheriff. He's been reelected a number of times.

In spite of being fired from the game wardens, I still remain friends with some of them. I try to keep track of what they are doing, and am sympathetic to the difficult job they have.

One of the best game wardens, in my opinion, was Art Allen. Art was a real gentleman, a tireless worker, a fine woodsman, and he was a good friend. Art loved to tie flies and fish with them for brook trout. I liked to do the same. We had some good fishing days together. Art's daughter, Gertrude, lives on Maple Hill.

Even though he had no choice but to arrest H.P., I think Charlie Ott is a very good game warden. Charlie and I stay in touch. His daughter, Shirley, married Terry Brownell, a local teacher. They soon moved to Tower where Terry became the school superintendent for many years.

Jack Linklater and Bill Hanson have retired at Ely, but I continue to hear good things about Jake Jacobsen, who's there now. That's a tough place to work out of, and he's done a good job. I know Benny Ambrose thinks a lot of Jake, and that's another good endorsement.

I have no hard feelings about any of the game wardens, with one exception that happened years later. They have a difficult job, and for the most part, they do it well. They deserve our gratitude and respect.

6

The Depression Years

In 1931, the Paine Hotel burned to the ground. It had been renamed the Tourist Hotel, but it was still the Paine to most of us. I was sorry to see the Paine Hotel burn, because it was a special place for Jo and me. It became occupied by the El Ray Restaurant, owned by Ray Sjoberg. It is now called the Blue Water Cafe.

After the stock market crash in 1929, things got bad quickly. Jobs disappeared. Prices for fur dropped way down. The fish and lumber markets were also terrible. These three categories drove everything we had in the county. Tourism was still in its infancy, but even then, people recognized it needed to grow.

Everyone was in trouble during the Depression. There were many who lost their jobs. Even though we lived in a massive game refuge, illegal trapping is how many of us managed to survive. The price of fur may have been way down, but at least you could still sell it for cash. During the early Depression years, the price for fisher pelts rose dramatically. Fur buyers would pay over a hundred dollars for fisher. They are marketed as sable, and make a beautiful and luxurious fur coat. We were told they were popular in Europe.

We developed a technique to run them down on snowshoes. We'd walk through the woods until we found a fresh fisher track. Then, we'd stay on it until we caught up to them. Tracking fisher through the alder swamps was the hardest because they would follow the numerous rabbit trails, and it was hard to sort out all the tracks. It could sometimes take two or three days before we caught them. It didn't matter. We'd stay on their track until we chased them into a hole or up a tree. If they were in a tree, we'd shoot them in the head with our .22 rifle. If they went into a hole, we'd build a barricade in front and set a trap in the one opening we'd left. Then we'd build a fire and smoke them out. Running fisher was exciting and rewarding. It was also hard on the snowshoes, and it seemed we were always breaking something. We carried wire and pliers to fasten splints to the ash frames as needed.

The two Hoffman brothers were very good woodsmen, and ran fisher like the rest of us. One winter, when the snow was deep and soft, they came out of the woods onto Alice Lake and spied two wolves not far down the shore. It was too far to shoot, but they thought they could run them down on snowshoes. They were in great physical shape from all their work chasing fisher. They told me the wolves started running, and stopped to shit once. After that, they really took off. Up near Knife Lake the Hoffman boys gave up the chase when it appeared the wolves were getting way ahead of them and were never going to stop. They had been chasing them in different directions for over forty miles.

Archie Jackson was another trapper who ran fisher. Archie said one time he was over the border in Canada at a place called Arrow Lake. Arrow Lake lies just to the east of Rose Lake. It's eighteen miles long, with a very narrow spot midway down the lake, so it's almost like two nine-mile-long lakes. The whole place is entirely in Canada. Archie was in the woods, somewhere along the west half of the lake, when he came across a fresh fisher track. He followed it for some time, and finally chased the fisher into a hole. It wasn't too far from the lakeshore. The more he investigated, the more it appeared to be a small cave. He blocked up the narrow entrance and left a small opening for his trap. He built a big, smudgy fire and kept throwing green spruce and balsam boughs on it. Finally, the thick smoke drove the fisher out and Archie caught it. Before he left, he investigated the cave and found it contained a cache of voyageur trading goods that were very old and in remarkably good shape. Archie was violating so many laws, he decided to get out of there while his luck still held. He has never been back. He wouldn't tell me any more details of the location, just that it was on the west half of the lake.

In later years, Archie became friends with Sister. She reported to me he told her the same story about discovering the small cave at

Arrow Lake, but that he told her it also contained silver. If that was true, I don't know why he didn't try to take some of it. Or, maybe he did, and just didn't want to admit it. In any event, it sounds like there is a cave there, with something important in it. I've often thought of trying to look for it, but that's just too much country to search.

The weather seemed to be especially bad during those years. One fall, I was trapping mink northeast of Alice Lake out of a cabin that is now long gone. I had a lot of traps set, and was catching a good number of mink. On November 8, we had three and a half feet of snow! Fortunately, I had snowshoes in the cabin. It was very difficult to find my traps, but I was determined to find them all and not waste one single animal. I found every trap. I had used mostly alder toggles to wire the traps to, and I could find the alder poles sticking above the snow. This reinforced a lesson I already knew. Be prepared for anything. I have never again seen snow like that in early November.

Although the era of the railroad logging was past, there were still many signs of their presence. Most of the logging camps included a sawmill to cut the logs into boards to decrease the costs of shipping. One of these was located on the South Brule River at Bower Trout Lake. There was a huge pile of slabs and lumber edgings that somehow had escaped burning. One year for mink trapping, I built a cabin there, using the edgings as the frame and covering it with slabs. This place was so tight it was mouse-proof. I really enjoyed it.

Bears have always created special problems for trappers. They like to tear things up. They will eat your food, wreck your camps, and rip the canvas on your canoe. They can be a real problem, but I have never been afraid of them or feared they would eat me. That is, except for one fall during the early 1930s. It was almost like the bears were going through their own difficult Depression that year. I'd see a lot of bears during the day. They would sometimes follow me all day and make me very nervous. At night, they'd climb on the roof of my cabin. I carried a gun, but never had to use it on a bear during this period. I never saw bears act this way in prior years, and I have never seen anything like it since.

People had a hard time paying their taxes during the Depression. Every time the local paper came out with a list of delinquent taxes, it seemed longer. So far, we had managed to get by. Because the county had less money coming in, they had to raise our property tax assessments. One year, the list of tax delinquencies was over eighty percent of all property owners. I got behind on my taxes too, but was always able to somehow catch up with the payment in time, and keep our house.

It was a very difficult time, not only for individuals, but also for the counties. The lack of property taxes coming in from private land, along with the huge amount of public land, made it hard for the county government to operate. I believe the county received no taxes, or any other kind of compensation, from any of the public lands during that time.

The game refuge was still in effect with its regulations enforced, but we trappers always tried to stay a step ahead of the game wardens. We developed tricks to try to fool them. One was to cut the soles out of an old pair of boots. When I came to a portage, I'd tie them on so that they pointed backward, and walk across with my tracks pointing opposite of the direction I was traveling.

It took most of the 1930s for things to get better. When conditions did improve, it happened more quickly here than many other counties in the rest of the state, probably because of all of our public land in Cook, Lake, and St. Louis counties. Federal money began to show up. Public works projects started to occur. First, it was for a new airport in Grand Marais, where the high school is located today. Right after that came many jobs to work on roads and bridges.

These jobs were all temporary. One summer, I worked at one, building the new Tourist Park downtown on the harbor. I really liked that because it was close to my house and sometimes I would walk home for lunch. Jobs like this, combined with my trapping income, were how I got by. It also fit a lifestyle I thoroughly enjoyed. Fur prices began to come back up, and there were more of us back trapping again.

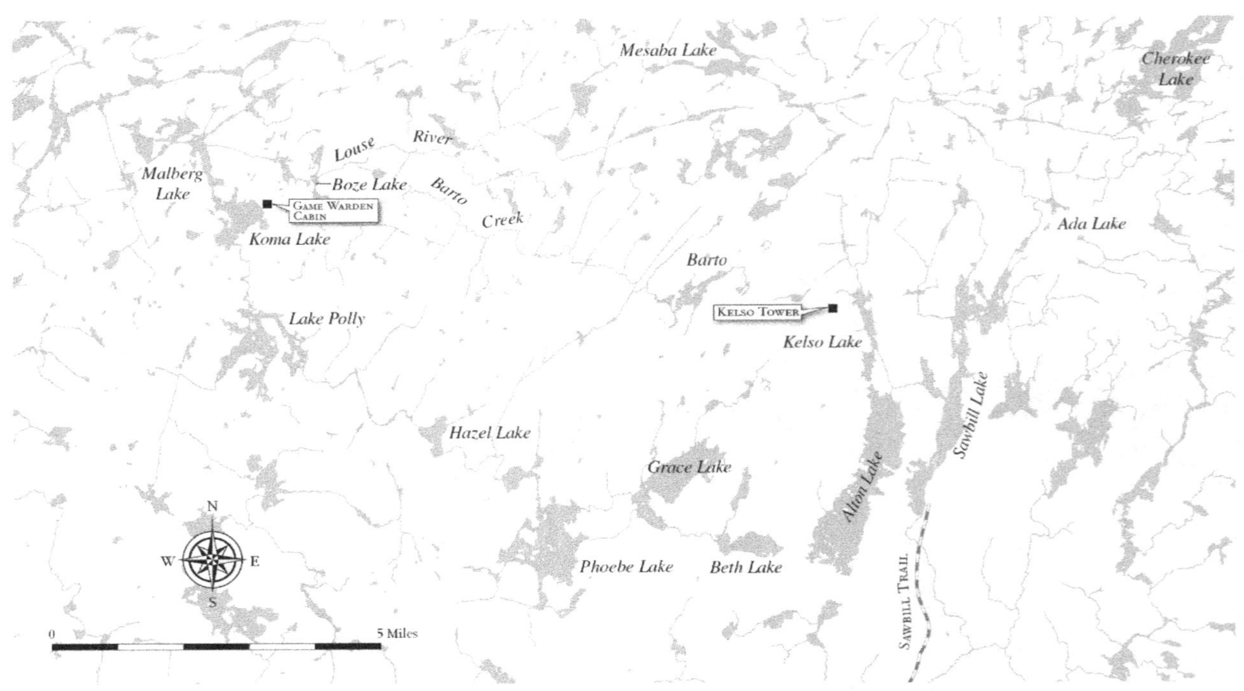

Mesaba Lake
Cherokee Lake
Louse River
Malberg Lake
Boze Lake
Barto
Game Warden Cabin
Creek
Ada Lake
Koma Lake
Barto
Kelso Tower
Lake Polly
Kelso Lake
Sawbill Lake
Hazel Lake
Grace Lake
Afton Lake
N
W E
S
Phoebe Lake
Beth Lake
Sawbill Trail
0
5 Miles

7

A Turtle Saves the Day

Seven cups of flour for seven days! That was the only food I had left. I wasn't starving, but I was very hungry. On the first of April, a small plane on skis dropped me at Barto Lake. I trapped beaver during the spring breakup. Now it was April 28. The plane was not due back until May 5. It would pick me up on open water down at Phoebe Lake, five miles to the south of my small camp.

Ernie Hautala, the pilot, was from Ely. Everyone called him "Hoot." Hoot specialized in flying outlaw trappers into the Superior Primitive Area and Quetico Provincial Park in Canada. Hoot was a tremendous pilot, a friend, and could always be depended on to pick you up when he said he would. So far as I know, he was never caught by the law.

This was during the Depression years, when the whole country was still the ill-conceived, massive state game refuge. It was up to nearly two million acres. Hoot did a good business flying trappers into it. There were many more of us than people realized, and we probably made the difference as to how Hoot was able to stay in business. It was also how we provided for our families. As I said before, we all barely managed to get by in those days.

If Hoot said he'd be there on May 5, he would be there unless really bad weather kept him from flying, or the ice had yet to go out. That would not be a problem this year. Hoot needed the much bigger lake to pick me up, because he'd have his two-seat plane on floats, and I would have a full planeload of beaver hides. We'd be heavy, and it would require a long takeoff run to get in the air. A regular day for Hoot; it should be no problem. That's what I hoped.

I chose the Barto country to trap in that spring for a number of reasons. There are many small lakes and streams, and it is off the beaten path. I didn't think anyone had been in there trapping in recent years, and beaver should be plentiful.

All that turned out to be true. I kept my fires small, and tried to burn only dry popple wood, which produces very little smoke. I camped off a small creek and went out of my way to leave as little sign in the country as possible. I carried a .22 pistol, but never fired a shot. Now that the snow was mostly gone, I was invisible unless somebody stumbled right over me.

A main canoe route goes through Phoebe Lake, and there was a good chance game wardens would patrol along it. Sawbill Lake is less than a day's walk to the east. It has road access from Tofte and a guard station that is used regularly by both federal rangers and state game wardens. In addition to Phoebe, some of the lakes on the way to Sawbill are named Beth, Grace, and Ella. Years earlier, Old Man Mulligan named them after his daughters. As a county surveyor, he got to assign names to unnamed features on maps.

In the opposite direction, the canoe route follows the Phoebe River going north. It empties into Polly Lake, then Koma, and up into the "Big Bend" country of Mahlberg Lake. There is a state game warden cabin on the east side of Koma. Because I had been a game warden years earlier, I knew these routes were regularly patrolled.

All in all, this Barto country was an ideal place to be. There were beaver everywhere and spring came quickly. I caught as many as I wanted in a couple of weeks. "As many as I wanted" was as much as I figured I could get into Hoot's plane. I made birch hoops to sew my beaver hides on, and when the weather was nice they would dry in two or three days.

There was a good load for the plane coming in. Beaver traps are heavy. In addition, I had an axe, ice chisel, a canvas tarp to sleep under and keep my hides dry, and other trapping and cooking gear. In my zeal to keep the weight down somehow the food came up short. I measured my remaining flour three times, and each time it came out to seven cups. Measuring it again wasn't going to make any more. There was a tiny bit of tea left, but that was it. I was stuck with what I had.

I cached the traps and nearly all the rest of my things at my camp. The hides were rolled into a bale, as tight as I could get them. I put the bale of hides in my big packsack along with the tarp, the remaining flour and tea, a frying pan, and a teapot. I planned to take only the beaver hides when I left Phoebe.

I shouldered my heavy pack and went south on the five-mile walk down to Phoebe. Flying in, Hoot and I picked a place on the north shore where he said he would return for me, and this is where I headed. I got down there with no trouble, and soon found the right spot on the shoreline. The problem was, I was a week early. Normally that would not be a problem. What trapper in the world wouldn't want a week of luxury in a beautiful setting in the sun while he waited to be picked up by plane and flown out to his car? My stomach sure didn't agree.

Spring comes to northern Minnesota in predictable ways. First, it always arrives from the west. A lake in the Ely region will lose its ice a week earlier than a similar-sized lake in the Gunflint Trail region. I don't know why this is. It's never been explained to me, but that's how it always happens. So, if Phoebe Lake was open, I knew the lakes around Ely would also be open.

Regardless of where it is located, an individual lake will always melt and lose its ice on the north shore first. The ice and snow on the south shore are always the last to go. This I understand, and it's easy to see why. The sun this time of the year is in the south. The north shore of a lake always receives the most sun on the ice. Also, the ground down to the lakeshore on the north side of a lake is a south-facing slope. It has a better angle to the sun and warms up first. It is not uncommon to have whole north sides of lakes bare while the south sides are still covered in snow.

The final thing to know about the ice going out in the spring is that rivers, beaver ponds, and smaller lakes always lose their ice before the bigger lakes do. The deepest and largest lakes like Knife, Saganaga, and Gunflint always lose their ice last.

My waiting spot on the north side of Phoebe demonstrated all of this. It was warming up. The ground was bare, the ice had melted a

Hoot Hautala with "Travel Air" airplane on skis. Jack Hautala

good distance out from shore, and spring was coming fast. In another day or two, Phoebe would be wide open. Even though foot travel on the lakes was now impossible, I was still wary of being discovered. If I could walk around on land in this country, so could a determined game warden. Therefore, I didn't try to find a partridge or beaver and shoot my pistol.

That first day down at the lake, I hid my beaver hides nearby and made a small camp, well away from the shoreline. I went down to the water's edge and just sat there, thinking. My stomach growled and I got hungrier and hungrier. There had to be something I could do for more food. Maybe I could go back for some of the twine I'd used with the beaver hoops and attach some kind of a homemade fishing hook. But what would I use for bait? Could I try to snare a fish or beaver? That didn't seem likely. I was stumped. I just sat there; I had to think of something.

When the afternoon was at its warmest, I saw a ripple in the

Hoot Hautala in flight. *Note famous grin.* Jack Hautala

water, and along came the biggest turtle I have ever seen. I remained very still, but my mind was racing. What could I do to capture him? I couldn't let him get away. The turtle slowly swam past me. On sudden impulse, I leaped into the waist deep water, caught the turtle, and threw it up on shore. I came out of that icy water quickly, and got the turtle farther away from the water's edge.

I was cold and wet. What should I do next? I'd never killed a turtle. I'd never even eaten turtle, but I heard they were good. Through trial and error, I killed and butchered the turtle. I was amazed at its size and all the different kinds of meat on it.

I built a small fire from dry popple, sliced off some strips of meat and fried it, while also drying my outer clothes. The turtle meat tasted great. My luck had changed. The god of trappers was with me that day. I iced the carcass down, and for seven days that turtle and my remaining flour kept me fed. It wasn't anything fancy, but it was enough.

On May 5, I was up early and ready for Hoot. True to his word, he showed up at midday. He remembered exactly where we agreed he would pick me up, landed close by, and taxied in. We didn't waste time talking. There would be plenty of time for that later. We just loaded my furs and took off. It was a very long takeoff run, but soon we were in the air. Hoot turned around and gave me that trademark grin of his.

Although his seaplane base was on Shagawa Lake at Ely, Hoot flew us to a small lake south of Vermillion Lake. From there he drove me to a place where my car was stored. The owner had food and coffee for us, and then wisely left us alone.

Hoot and I talked. One really interesting thing he said was, "Alec, about the time I dropped you off this spring, I had to take a trapper to a lake farther east. I dropped him off right about dark. On the night flight back to Ely, I counted twelve campfires from trappers."

Flying in the dark was not unusual at all for Hoot. That flight, along one course on one night, confirmed that there were a lot of us out there. I've never forgotten that number.

I wanted to talk with him about the coming fall. "Hoot, I hear Isle Royale is full of mink and they need to be thinned out. I think most everyone but a few fishing families will be gone by late October, and I'll pretty much have the place to myself. Will you fly me out there?"

He grinned at me and thought for a while. "I'm not worried about getting caught, but there are special things about this that bother me. Because of the long distance, I'll have to cache extra gas somewhere along the route. Also, as you know, the weather out on Lake Superior in the fall can be very different from the weather in Ely. You might be stranded there for a long time, waiting for me."

We talked about the problems a little longer. Hoot ended by saying, "Right now, I'm not ready to promise to fly you out there. Let me think about it over the summer and I'll get back to you."

True to his word, Hoot got a message to me later during the summer. It was in code, but it meant he had decided it just wouldn't work. I didn't try to change his mind. I figured I might have used up my supply of good luck with the turtle, and didn't want to push it.

8

The CCCs

In the 1930s, President Roosevelt created a program called the Civilian Conservation Corps, or the CCC. It was an employment program for young men. This was part of Roosevelt's "New Deal" to fight the Depression. It went on to become something even more important than that.

The CCC program came into northeastern Minnesota very quickly. CCC camps were built throughout the National Forest. The Forest Service provided a long list of jobs to the camp superintendents and supervised the overall operation. The camp superintendents assigned the jobs to the foremen of the crews. The boys on the crews got the jobs done. In the state forests out of Ely, Finland, and Hovland, the same thing occurred. Even Isle Royale had a CCC camp.

A CCC enrollee was paid $30 per month, plus free room and board. Free work clothing was also provided, including good wool coats, winter boots, hats, and mittens. Young men from outside the area showed up by the hundreds. There were also jobs for local young men if they wanted to become a "CC boy." (Most of us soon shortened their title to "CCs," and the two- and three-letter versions were used interchangeably.) Older local men could become foremen of the crews or do some of the many other jobs necessary to support the massive operation. These jobs paid forty-five dollars per month. The Army ran the camps, which had about 150 enrollees in them. The whole thing had a military feel to it. Evidence of their work is everywhere today. I can't possibly tell you everything that was accomplished; preparing to fight forest fires has to be at the top of the list.

The CCs built fire lookout towers that covered all of northern Minnesota. Most were about one hundred feet high. They were constructed from heavily-galvanized angle-iron that was bolted together using predrilled holes. They went up by hand. They didn't need heavy equipment like a crane, or even electricity, to work on them. All towers were pretty much the same, except for some variation in the height. Once you had worked on one tower, you knew the others would go up the same way.

Construction of these towers was a huge undertaking. Getting the very heavy steel to the tower location was a big problem. Some locations could be driven to, but others were far from any roads. They were each located on top of the highest hill in the area. The tower sites in the Superior Primitive Area were the most difficult to get the steel to. The Kekekabic tower was by far the hardest, but the Kelso tower was also very difficult.

Lookout towers were connected by a single-wire telephone line to their nearest neighboring tower and also back to town. Thick, single-strand, galvanized wire was used. It was flexible and very strong. The wire was attached to glass insulators, which were usually nailed to live trees. CC boys were assigned in teams of two to man the towers and keep the phone lines working. There were many problems with these phone lines due to falling trees or bull moose getting their antlers tangled in them if the wire dipped down.

A cabin was constructed for each lookout tower. They were usually located near a lake for boat and canoe access. These cabins were good-sized, and sometimes housed "smoke chasers," who responded to lightning strikes. Other times, the cabins were used by Forest Service rangers or state game wardens doing other work in the area. Many of them were expanded over time, and became known as guard stations.

The Kelso cabin north of Sawbill was not located near a canoe route. However, the CCs built a good trail from the tower and cabin site down to Kelso Lake. At the lake, they built a rugged wooden box complete with a hinged top and a lock. It was about twenty feet long, and was used to store a canvas canoe. With their canoe in the box and the lid locked shut, the canoe was safe from bears. That old box is in pretty poor condition, but it's still there today.

Where there were no roads, good trails were built between towers. The telephone lines followed these trails, and this helped with maintenance of the lines. The forty-four-mile Kekekabic Trail is the longest. It connects the Fernberg tower near Lake One east of Ely to the Kekekabic tower, to the Gunflint tower north of Grand Marais.

Another trail was built south from the Kekekabic tower to the tower at Kelso Mountain. From there the trail and telephone line connected to the cabin on Sawbill and the phone line to Tofte.

The Kekekabic tower and the lake downhill to the north of it lie in the middle of the Superior Primitive Area. It is a long way from the Fernberg Road out of Ely, the Gunflint Trail out of Grand Marais, and the Sawbill Trail out of Tofte. The trails leading to this area are all difficult due to some very high water crossings that are impassable in the spring. I've spent quite a bit of time back there. The river crossing at the outlet of Gabimichigami Lake was by far the worst. Today, the Forest Service has relocated the trail north to Agamok Gorge, where they built a bridge over the river.

Another big program accomplished by the CCs in our area was for recreation. It is apparent that the big picture here was to create a fourth leg to our economy's three-legged stool of logging, commercial fishing, and trapping. You can see evidence of this recreation work everywhere today.

The CCs built roads and bridges. They constructed campgrounds and hiking trails. They built boat landings and put up nice informational signs for visitors.

They improved the main canoe routes within the Superior Primitive Area, as well as throughout the rest of the border country. They built new campsites and rock fireplaces for safe campfires. They constructed beautiful log picnic tables in many of the campsites.

For the main canoe routes, crews of CC boys transported wheelbarrows in their canoes. They located gravel sources, and built up a nice, wide tread on the portage trails. They constructed small boat docks at each end of the portage and made certain there were no rocks leading in to them. These actions have prolonged the life of many a canoe.

The CCs carefully measured the length of each portage. They installed informational signs at each end to inform visitors of their location and the length of the trail. Someone decided the length of a portage should be measured in rods, and this is what is used on the signs and maps. I knew from my days working with the surveyors on the boundary survey that a rod is sixteen and a half feet. There are four rods to a chain, and eighty chains to a mile. So, 320 rods equals a mile. It is common lingo for surveyors and foresters, but it took some getting used to for the rest of us.

One year there was a major accident involving the CCs on Sawbill Lake. A barge sank in deep water. No one was injured, but almost everything on board sank and was never recovered. Suddenly, every piece of accountable federal property that had ever been missing on the Superior National Forest was said to have been on that barge. The Forest Service guys said it solved a lot of their administrative problems.

The CCs did a lot of forest management work. They planted, thinned, and pruned trees. They built roads into the forest and did many other things to improve their condition. They also helped the state with fish and wildlife work, like conducting lake and stream surveys. Then they stocked everything from brook trout to walleyes in many of the lakes, as directed by the DNR. The CCs improved trout streams by creating pools and other habitats. They gathered massive amounts of wild rice and planted it in many places. A lot of that rice took, one good example being the wild rice in the Upper Temperance River country.

They also conducted wildlife management surveys. One of their studies showed that there were more beaver in some areas outside the massive game refuge than there were inside. The areas outside were open to trapping while the refuge was supposed to be closed. This new information proved that we trappers had been right from the beginning about the behavior of animals. However, it didn't change anything regarding the prohibition on trapping in the main part of the refuge until the 1950s.

I was too old to work on a CCC crew and I never got to supervise one. But when I wasn't trapping, I had a lot of part-time jobs for the Forest Service during these years. I mostly repaired their fire pumps and outboard motors. There are two types of fire pumps. One is for one-inch-diameter hose, which seem to break down a lot. The other is for one-and-a-half-inch hose. These are called "Wye" pumps and are more reliable. They also deliver a lot more water to fires. I did most of my repair work on outboard motors and fire pumps at the district ranger station in Grand Marais. Once in a while they would send me to work on something out of town.

There were some big forest fires in 1935. The CCC was still in its infancy, but the CCs helped to get the fires controlled. The biggest year for fires the area has ever experienced was in 1936. There was a long drought and record high temperatures that summer. On top of that, there was a lot of dry lightning. Thankfully, the network of fire lookout towers was in place and the CC boys were in their camps. Most of the fires were spotted from the newly constructed towers, and the CCs were dispatched to fight them.

Some of the fires started in Canada and came south over the border. We all got involved in trying to stop those. My brother, Charlie, and I worked fighting the fires for over a month straight. We were on the American side of North Lake on a state forestry fire, a particularly bad one. My friend, Patty Bayle, was the ranger in charge. Charlie and I witnessed a burning piece of birch bark blown a one-mile-distance across the lake from the Canadian side. It started a fire on our side that we were able to put out, but it hardly made a difference. The fires became so bad, they had to close the Gunflint Trail for over six weeks that summer. More than eight hundred men were fighting the fires just along the Gunflint Trail region. Some of the lakes became covered with ash.

The Superior Primitive Area was also hit hard. One fire started behind Frost Lake and burned east, almost to the edge of Long Island Lake. It burned for a long time. Two hundred CCC men were initially sent to fight it, but their numbers were soon more than tripled. Forest Service rangers led half of the initial attack force down a hastily bulldozed three-mile trail to Rib Lake. Then, they walked the fire fighters cross-country down to Long Island. From there they continued cross-country to get to the fire. I still use their old trail along the north side of Auke Lake, west of Long Island. The other hundred men on initial attack were sent up from Sawbill and went to Frost Lake. Eventually, seven hundred men were needed to control this fire.

Another big fire started at Cherokee Lake and went east, nearly to Brule Lake. The Forest Service cabin on the north side of Cherokee almost burned. It was saved in the nick of time by men in a floatplane who brought in a fire pump and hose from Sea Gull Lake. More than six hundred men were needed to fight this fire. There was one fatality. A firefighter named Jerry McDonald died from drowning in Sitka Lake when his canoe overturned. McDonald's regular job was superintendent of the Sawbill CCC camp. He'd been working hard on the fire line for over a week, and the Forest Service guys thought he didn't have the strength to swim to shore when his canoe tipped over.

There was also a big fire off the Sawbill Trail. Another big one called the Hog Lake fire burned above the railroad grade south of Brule Lake. Johnny Blackwell supervised a crew of CCC men on that one. At one time, seventeen fires were burning. Most of the fires smoldered and burned until winter, but eventually they had control lines around their perimeters.

Everyone agreed the CCC had made the difference. These men were treated like heroes, and they deserved every bit of recognition.

Following the terrible fire season of 1936, the winter was very bad. The snow was exceptionally deep and the winds seemed to blow all the time, causing severe drifting. County road crews had a difficult time keeping the main roads open. One crew was gone from home for over a week, trying to keep the highway open to the west as far as Cramer. They would plow all day and then sleep at the nearest house. With all the snow, there was also a severe deer die-off that winter.

By the end of the 1930s, there was a new concern. There was war in Europe and fear it might spread. When Pearl Harbor happened and the United States went to war, it was apparent that the CCC program had prepared many of our young men. They had been away from home and lived in army camps and barracks. They had fought forest fires. They understood discipline and knew how to take orders. They became good soldiers.

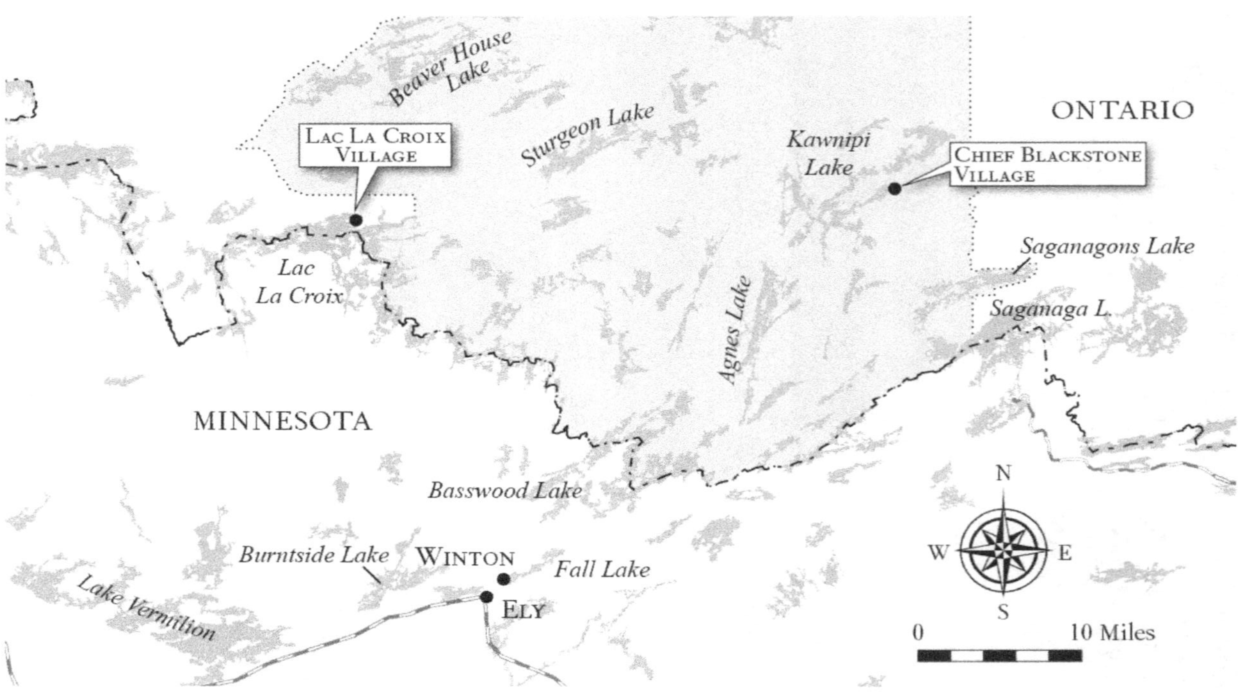

Beaver House Lake
Lac La Croix Village
Lac La Croix
Sturgeon Lake
ONTARIO
Kawnipi Lake
Chief Blackstone Village
Saganagons Lake
Saganaga L.
Agnes Lake
MINNESOTA
Basswood Lake
Burntside Lake
Winton
Fall Lake
Lake Vermilion
Ely
N
W
E
S
0
10 Miles

9

The Indians

The Indians here are called Chippewa by most white people. Ojibwe is another name given them. The Indians call themselves "Anishinabe." It means "original people." There were isolated families of Indians scattered along the border. They had to move with the seasons to find food. There were also Indian villages along the North Shore of Lake Superior, but with a few exceptions, there were no villages north in the interior.

The Anishinabe have no written history produced by themselves. Stories are passed down, generation to generation, in the oral tradition. One common story is that the Anishinabe migrated to this country from the east, to this wonderful land where "food grows on the water" (wild rice).

While working for the International Boundary Commission, I was able to meet and get to know many Indian people on both sides of the border. I'm using their English names, but they all have Indian names. Later, I married a girl who is half Indian. I have trapped, fished, hunted, and lived around Indian people my entire life.

There were times when I went on trips beyond the actual border lakes we were surveying. While at Saganaga Lake, I was assigned to help two boatloads of people on a trip into Canada. We went to Jack Powell's place on the northeast end of Saganagons Lake. The two men in charge of the project wanted to meet Powell to get his views on the actual location of the boundary across Saganaga. My job was to help carry the boats, motors, and other gear over the half-mile portage around Silver Falls on the big river connecting the two lakes.

Saganagons is nearly as long as Saganaga. It lies to the north of, and parallel to, Saganaga. "Sag-in-ah-gah" means "twisting lake with many islands." Someone claimed there are 360 islands on Saganaga.

I don't know about that, but there are a lot of them. Saganagons has nowhere near that many islands, but there are a lot of them there, too. The difference between the two similar Indian names has to do with the smaller size of Saganagons. "Gonz," or "gance," means little. It is beautiful country and easy to see why Jack Powell settled there.

Powell was a second-generation Irishman, an American citizen. I don't know what became of his US citizenship status with all his years in Canada. He has passed on. In the late 1800s, he came to Ely from Michigan. He tried working in the mines and logging camps, but couldn't find a job he liked. In 1901, he married eighteen-year-old Mary Ottertail, who was originally from the Lac La Croix village. John Ottertail was her father. Mary was living on the Canadian side of Basswood Lake when she met Jack. He was working on a logging train near Ely. After they married, the tribe held a shaking wigwam ceremony at Lac La Croix and told her she was no longer a member.

Jack Powell and Mary moved over to Saganagons. They lived way down at the east end of the lake, just five miles above the northeast arm of Saganaga. This may have been the location of an old trading post. Powell knew he was in Canada, but he built cabins and raised his family there, anyway. Sometime after the Quetico Park was created, he became a ranger for them. Jack never learned to speak Ojibwe and Mary never learned English. They somehow communicated with no problems, and their five children grew up speaking both languages.

Chief Blackstone One was key to passing the 1873 treaty, the third treaty between Canada and the Indians in this part of Ontario. He was Chief of the Lac La Croix village at this time. Although he took part in the negotiations, Chief Blackstone One, along with two other chiefs, refused to sign the treaty. Later, they signed some kind of amendment to it. Ojibwe stories say Chief Blackstone One was a great orator. He formed alliances with the Sioux to prevent the white man from taking their land, and he may even have traveled to England. Chief Blackstone One had three wives before his death.

Chief Blackstone Two was a powerful and widely known chief in the Quetico Park region and beyond. He lived in a village located at a place called Kawa Bay on Kawnipi Lake. It's about twenty-five miles downstream and north of Saganagons. The village site was located behind a sand beach at the head of the bay, just south of where the Wawiag River comes in. There were approximately twenty-five families living there at the time of our trip to Powell's. Chief Blackstone Two lived in a cabin, and all the other families lived either in wigwams covered with birch bark, or teepees covered with stretched moose hides. Chief Blackstone Two had seven wives during his lifetime.

Today this is all within the Quetico Provincial Park, which was established in 1913. It's on a well-known canoe route called the "Hunters Island Route." I've been there. Kawa Bay has a lot of wild rice. Because of the abundance of fish and wild rice, it's easy to see why it has long been the site of an Indian village.

Our head people met and visited with Jack Powell at his home on Sagangons. I was not part of any of the discussions, and was free to wander around. I met Jack's three sons, Mike, Frank and Billy. They were not much different in age from me. I also met their two sisters, Esther and Tempest. Esther is the oldest of the five children and Tempest is the youngest. Over the years, I have remained friends with the boys. They said Chief Blackstone Two was home at Kawnipi. I wish I could have met him.

During the winter of 1919, a terrible sickness swept through Chief Blackstone Two's village at Kawa Bay. Tragedies like this had happened before in the border country. The official story is it was a "flu epidemic." Many of the Indians blame the Jesuit missionaries for deliberately introducing smallpox via blankets they provided to them. They believe the Jesuits sometimes did this purposely when the Indians refused to convert to Christianity and instead retained their "pagan beliefs." It is well known that Chief Blackstone was the main reason most of the Indians in the region had refused to convert. He refused to allow his people to do so.

All but two of the men and most of the women and children in the village had become very sick. Chief Blackstone was one of the two men not affected. The two of them, along with one of Blackstone's wives, left to get help. First, they headed for the Powell's place on

Saganagons. They hoped to use the Quetico Park shortwave radio there. They made it safely that far, but learned the batteries for the radio were dead. Next, they headed for Joe Russell's store and post office in Winton. They had Joe wire a message to Ottawa, asking for help. Joe's message said, "The Indian village at Kawa Bay is dying." There was no response and no one came to help.

They started right back. They chose the more direct route from Winton to Kawnipi by going up through Basswood to Agnes Lake. Along the way, the old chief became sick and died. They had to leave his body on the north shore of Agnes. It was later recovered by other Indians from Lac La Croix and given a proper burial. This included construction of a small grave house and fence. It was very important to build it at that spot, because Anishinabe people believe if their bones are disturbed, their spirit can never be at rest. Over the years since then, the gravesite has been found by canoeists and looted. In spite of this, I hope Blackstone's spirit is at peace.

Some people believe Chief Blackstone took to his grave the secret location of more gold in the area. There have always been trace amounts of gold in the border country. There is even a working gold mine north of Kawnipi near the town of Kenora. The location of that mine is believed to have been provided by Chief Blackstone. I never paid much attention to these rumors, and thought with Blackstone's death the rumors of gold had ended. Later, I found out I was wrong.

I wish we would have been working between Basswood and Saganaga during the time Chief Blackstone went for help. We might have been able to help him. Unfortunately, our job along there was finished.

The story of Chief Blackstone, his tragic death and that of his people, spread throughout the border region. Coming on the heels of the Cloquet Fire disaster that previous fall, it was the second bad event to occur in a short period. It marked the end of the village at Kawa Bay. In that location and others within the Quetico Park, the Provincial Government has forcibly evicted the Indians, some even at gunpoint during the winter, to locations outside the park. This happened even though both sides had signed the treaty in 1873 establishing the reserves. There are some terrible stories. Many of the Indians went to the village located just outside the park on the Canadian side of Lac La Croix Lake. Today there are no Indians left inside the park. *Author's note: In 1991, the Province of Ontario issued a formal apology to the descendants of the Indian people of the Quetico, providing further credibility to these stories. Their struggles have been astounding.*

I firmly believe the Indian people on the Canadian side of the border had, and still have, conditions much more difficult than those on the US side. However, this distinction makes it sound like there is a formal line and you live on one side or the other. There is now, but Indian people along the border had always been free to move from one side to the other. Today, Indian families have to choose which country to live in. A few still manage to keep a foot in each.

One winter, I trapped out of Grand Marais with a partner named Alex Wishcop. Alex was a fine man. He's gone now. He was an Indian originally from the Indian village at Beaver Bay. From there, trails used for hundreds of years came down from Vermillion Lake, Basswood Lake, and Ely. Once I asked Alex what his last name meant. He said "sweet."

Alex married a woman named Adelaide. She is the daughter of Elizabeth Maymauskowaush, who is a sister to Jane Maymauskowaush, my mother-in-law. Adelaide and my wife, Jo, are first cousins and good friends.

Anishinabe call the rabbit "wabos." Alex showed me a technique he learned from his uncle for snaring rabbits. Once you catch one, cut the head off, and being careful not to get blood on anything, rub the clean rabbit head on your snares. Do not use your bare hands on the head, or it will pick up your smell. The rabbit head makes the snares smell as if other rabbits have passed through them, and you will catch more rabbits.

One winter we trapped out of a cabin up on Ball Club Lake. Our luck was terrible. We couldn't seem to catch a thing. We pulled our traps for the time being, left our gear in the cabin, and returned to our families in town.

After a few days, it was time to go back, but I could not find Alex anywhere. Adelaide thought he was with me. Finally, I left Grand Marais and snowshoed back up to Ball Club. I arrived at the cabin late in the afternoon and discovered Alex had already been there. He'd taken the Airtight stove and pulled out to trap alone, farther north at Bower Trout. It was a cold night for me with no stove. I started back for town in the morning.

I later learned what happened from Jo's Indian mother. Alex had gone up to Grand Portage to see Alex Posey, the medicine man. Wishcop hoped to learn from Posey why our trapping success was so poor. Posey was highly regarded, and Indians came from far and wide to seek his advice. Wishcop gave him tobacco and other gifts. After a shaking wigwam ceremony, Posey told him we were doing everything wrong. Posey reminded Wishcop that Anishinabe were always in close touch with the spirits. You are supposed to put something down on Mother Earth, such as a gift of tobacco to the Creator. When you catch an animal, you always first give thanks to its spirit for helping you. Posey wanted to know if we were doing any of this. The answer was no. Alex Wishcop knew he'd never be able to explain these things to me, and more importantly, get me to follow them. So, he went off on his own.

Over the years as I continue to learn more about the Indians, I realize they divide into three groups. There are those who have adopted Christianity and given up their traditional ways. Most of the Indians are now in this group. A smaller group still tries to keep some of their old ways. But there are still a few who believe in, and follow, the old ways. This way of life is called the Midewiwin religion.

"Midewiwin" means "Grand Medicine Society." It is not usually talked about openly. It's a blend of both religion and medicine, and practitioners can attain various levels. The higher level you attain, the more information is revealed to you. Some of it is basic, like learning that birch bark tea can sometimes cure constipation. Other parts are more complex, such as learning about the royal fern, where to find it, and how to both gather and use it for certain ailments such as arthritis.

Walter and Alma Caribou. GRAND PORTAGE TRIBAL COUNCIL

There was an Indian village at Jackfish Bay on Basswood Lake, and within it was a very old ceremonial "big drum." The Gunflint Lake Indians, such as the Cooks and the Spoons, remember traveling there with their parents for pow wows, which were held in a popple dance ring. There is also an Indian cemetery near this old village site.

Walter Caribou now lives at Grand Portage. His experiences are also helpful in understanding what life was like for the Indians. Walter is not sure where, or when, he was born. His father was originally from Grand Portage and Chippewa City. Walter is descended from "Ah Dik" who was also called Chief Cariboo, one of the Indian chiefs who signed the 1854 Treaty. "Ah Dikonce," also known as Little Cariboo, was his son and went on to become chief. Swamper Cariboo is a cousin to Walter.

Walter's dad was looking for work and heard Indian people from Basswood could be hired as loggers around Ely. His dad went to the Basswood Lake area by following the centuries-old trail from Beaver Bay, where other cousins lived. Walter's first memories are being with his parents on Basswood. In those days, it was hard to find enough to eat during the winter. All the people in a village could easily kill all the animals nearby, so they broke up into small family units for the winter. It was a very hard life. In the spring, groups of these small families would come back together and literally count noses to see who had made it through the winter.

Walter remembers one event at a bay on Basswood Lake like it happened yesterday. It was during the late winter. Walter's father and uncle had gone hunting, and had planned to check on a family living in another bay about three miles away. They had seen no sign of them for several weeks. They arrived at their camp to investigate, and looked into their wigwam.

"Oh Yai! Windigo Kahn!" his father screamed out. The parents had turned into Windigos, human flesh eaters, who were possessed. They had eaten their children. Someone who has turned into a Windigo gains tremendous powers and is out of control.

Walter's father and uncle raced back to their wigwam, very frightened and excited. They told his mother they had to pack and leave immediately. They heard something outside. The two Windigos had followed them back and now wanted their children! Walter's mother covered her little boy and girl with a blanket and told them not to look out. They were crying. Walter peeked out from under his blanket. He stared outside and saw the Windigos. They looked terrible. They had eaten their fingernails and their fingers were raw and bleeding.

Walter's father grabbed his gun. He shot and thought he had killed the Windigo man. The woman escaped and was never seen again.

"Hurry up," Walter's dad said, "build a fire!"

They built a big fire. The Windigo man's body moved and Walter's dad shot him again. "Throw him in the fire!" his dad shouted. They threw him in the fire and the Windigo screamed out. They threw more and more dry logs over the body. The fire got bigger and bigger. Then they heard a strange sound come out of the Windigo and saw a big piece of ice come out of his body near his heart.

They didn't sleep that night, and as soon as it was daylight they packed up and left as fast as they could. As Walter grew up, he learned more about Windigos. A person can become a Windigo only in the winter. It is very difficult to kill one. It has happened a number of times in generations past. There was one at Grand Portage, another at Saganaga, and another one earlier on Basswood Lake. Details about the Grand Portage incident are still passed down in stories. That Windigo had been extremely difficult to kill. Walter still has his father's gun that was used to kill the Windigo on Basswood Lake. He has been back there, and reports nothing will grow at the spot where they killed the Windigo.

Like Jack Powell, Walter also married a woman from the Lac

Chief Mike Flatte, hereditary chief of the Grand Portage Band. *Note peace medals provided to an earlier chief prior to the War of 1812.*
COOK COUNTY HISTORICAL SOCIETY

LaCroix village. Alma Red Sky Geezhik is her name and she is a descendant of Chief Blackstone Two. They raised their children and lived for a long time in her village on the Canadian side of Lac La Croix. They still have many relatives living there. Walter has traveled all along the border country, trapping, hunting, and fishing. Today, he and Alma have moved to Grand Portage. I don't think Walter is any older than I am, so it's not that long ago when the Windigo event on Basswood Lake happened.

Life on the reservations on the US side of the border has also been hard for the Indians. It is much better today, but during the Depression years it was very difficult. Things got so bad at Grand Portage one year that the county commissioners wrote a letter to Washington, D.C., asking for emergency help for the Indians. This was during the time the county was having serious financial troubles of its own, so it must have been really bad at Grand Portage.

Congress passed a law in 1934, called the Indian Reorganization Act. It did away with the power of the hereditary chiefs. The law requires elections to a tribal council form of government on all reservations throughout the US. The Bureau of Indian Affairs made sure the reservations complied. At Grand Portage, Mike Flatte was chief. Mike still has the elaborate peace medals given to his relatives by the British. Mike's authority did not diminish overnight, and he retains great influence there, even today.

Over the years, I have made many Indian friends. I watched the Plummer kids from Gunflint grow up. George married Louise, a white woman from Minneapolis. They are raising their family in Grand Marais and live up the dead-end street near Jo and me. George continues to trap where his father did, north of Gunflint Lake in Canada. Lillian still lives at the old Plummer place on the Canadian side of Gunflint Lake and is good friends with Justine Kerfoot.

Walter Plummer, the third-oldest, died there on the Canadian side of Gunflint under suspicious circumstances. It was in a house fire that occurred during the middle of the night. Although his body was badly burned, his head had been split with an axe. Walter was rumored to have known Chief Blackstone's secret about the location of more gold. I still do not believe this. However, he may have been tortured for information. Provincial police did a poor job investigating his death.

I think the stories about the gold were firmly believed by some. Years after Walter's death, Charlie Cook, a cousin to the Plummers and a neighbor from farther down the shore, said he saw a white man, whom we all know, come out of the woods near Walter's place at about ten o'clock the next morning. This man still lives around here. As far as I know, Charlie was never questioned by anyone about Walter's death.

The Powell children have also grown up. Both Frank and Billy spent a lot of time around the town of Tower, which is located west of Ely. Frank married first one, and then another, sister from the Bruneau family there. Billy also married a Bruneau girl. There are six girls and four boys in that family. In the late 1920s, Frank and

Billy learned to fly and repair airplanes there from Dusty Rhoades on Vermillion Lake. Frank went on to get his Canadian pilot license. Billy got his license as a Canadian aircraft engineer, which is what their aircraft mechanics are called.

Both Frank and Billy built resorts on the Canadian side of Saganaga, and have raised their families as Canadians. Frank's resort is on the northeast arm of Saganaga where a five-mile trail runs north to the east end of Saganagons and comes out near his parents' home. Frank has always had an airplane he uses at his resort. Mike married Sophie, a granddaughter of Chief Blackstone Two. He guided on Saganaga, and tried his hand at logging. He also worked some for the Forest Service. His children are grown and now live in Grand Marais. Tempest stayed at Saganagons for a long time, taking care of her parents. Today, she lives on Saganaga.

We have all gone through big changes in our lives. As a child growing up in Milaca, I would never have imagined what would happen to me. The Indian people have experienced far greater changes in their lives.

10

WWII and the Years Immediately Following

World War II brought huge changes to our region. Gas rationing was strictly enforced. We had long distances to drive, so this hit us especially hard. At first, our gas rationing cards entitled us to only four gallons per week, but was increased because of the long distances we had to drive and all the special hardships it created. Tourism almost completely disappeared. If someone did want to come up here to visit, it was very difficult for them to do so.

Forest rangers were called up for military service. Others were sent off on lengthy assignments to the west coast or southeast Alaska where they helped obtain Sitka spruce. The wood was urgently needed for airplane and glider wings.

The CC boys in the fire towers quickly disappeared. Now women took responsibility at many of the towers and they did a fine job. It is fortunate that we experienced no big forest fires during this period, because our ready source of firefighters was gone. The big fires seem to come in cycles. We were, and still are, in a low period.

The poor resort owners had a very difficult time holding on to their businesses. Many had to close them up and leave during the war years. Charlie and Petra hunkered down at their resort on Clearwater and were somehow able to get by. At Gunflint Lake, Justine and Bill Kerfoot were able to keep their resort as well.

Up on Saganaga, Frank Powell had named his Canadian fishing resort Green Forest Lodge. It was beyond the end of the road and few visitors could get there. His brother Billy's resort, the Chippewa Inn Resort, was no different. They both had no visitors during that time. Frank closed Green Forest Lodge and moved to Minneapolis for work. Billy had to close his resort as well and moved to Grand Marais, where he was able to find work during the war years.

For those of us too old to be drafted, well-paying jobs seemed impossible to find around home. However, there were good jobs in Minneapolis and St. Paul. Like many others, that's where I had to go. I worked for a company called Mid-Continent Airlines, at their modification center for military aircraft. I got a job helping make aluminum parts that were designed by their engineers. We worked long hours, at least six days a week. Sometimes we'd even work seven days and get every other Sunday off. I saved my money and bought war bonds, just like everyone else.

I saw a few people I knew from northern Minnesota during this time. I recall visiting with Frank Powell and Dorothy Bruneau one Sunday afternoon. They were working for the Swift Meat Packing Company in St. Paul.

Jo's mother, Jane, died in 1941. She was seventy-nine years old. Two years later, in 1943, Jo's dad, Sam Zimmerman died. He was ninety-one. The deaths of her parents were hard on Jo. Sister was also very close to her grandparents, and grieved the loss.

I missed Jo and my girls. I was able to get home on the bus once in a while. They managed to get to Minneapolis to visit me. They moved down for a time, but had to go back for the girls to attend school. Sister came back and stayed with me near the end. Not only did I miss my family, I also terribly missed the country I had to leave behind.

While working at Mid-Continent with all that aluminum, I learned that some of it could be heated to a molten condition and poured in molds. During off-hours, I created the special skinning knife I still use today. I got hold of a high-quality file used by automobile body shops. It has exceptionally hard steel. Over time, I slowly worked that file into the shape of a knife, being very careful not to overheat it and destroy the temper. For a handle, I tapered it down and poured molten aluminum around it. My mold was a raw potato. It's not the most beautiful knife in the world, but there is nothing that will hold an edge like it. It replaced the fine-quality, old

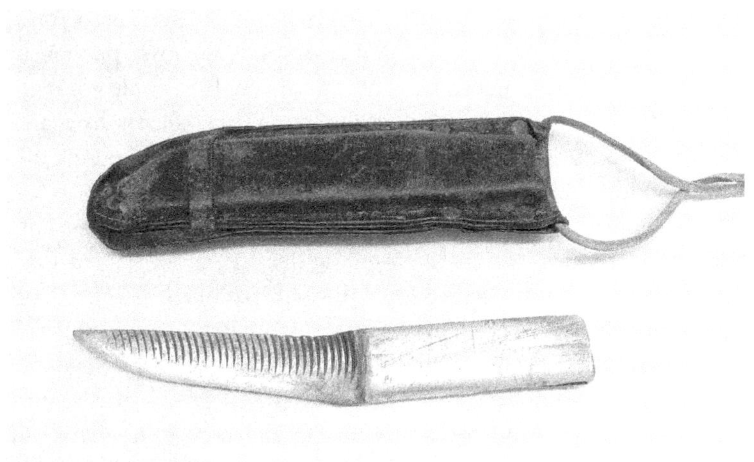

Beaver skinning knife made from an auto body file. *Note handle made by pouring molten aluminum into a raw potato mold.* Jack Blackwell

Marble knife I had long used. This knife project let me dream about the north country, and how well that knife would perform when I returned.

The Superior Primitive Area must have seen few people during the war. There were not many trappers around. When I finally returned, I found that beaver populations had greatly increased. It appeared no one had been trapping them, plus their food supply had really improved in the areas that experienced the big forest fires in the 1930s.

Charlie and Petra sold Clearwater Lodge at the end of the war. Their ten children, who had done most of the upkeep of the place, were grown and mostly gone. All of the work now fell on Charlie and Petra's shoulders. They were tired and it was time for a change. They sold the lodge to Art Schliep, but kept a pretty piece of lakeshore nearby for their new home, and enough other lakeshore property for some cabin sites for their children. Charlie immediately went to work on their new log home near the lodge.

After the war ended, it was like a switch was thrown and many things returned as they had been. However, there were also some big changes. Soldiers returned. Some of the CC boys, previously from out of the area, moved back here permanently. People got married and started families. They bought cars. There were jobs again. Everyone was optimistic, and had money to spend. Tourism took off. Visitors returned to the resorts.

Aluminum canoes, and then boats, appeared. They instantly became popular. The canoes were lighter and more rugged than their wood and canvas predecessors. Building canoes became a good side-business for the Grumman Aircraft Company now that the aluminum was not critically needed for aircraft.

The price paid for beaver skyrocketed. Although the absurd game refuge regulations prohibiting trapping were still in effect, old trappers resumed trapping, and new trappers appeared. For a year or two in the late 1940s, fur buyers were paying one dollar per inch for beaver! This price didn't last for many years, and has never been reached again.

You have to understand how beaver pelts are graded and measured. A stretched and dried hide is measured in inches. First, the length from its nose to the end of the fur where the tail has been cut off is measured. Next, the fur buyer measures the width of the hide. The two numbers are added together. This determines the beaver's size. An average size is around sixty-three inches, but there is a lot of variation.

A "blanket," the term you hear people talk about a lot, is between sixty-five and seventy inches. A "super blanket" is greater than seventy inches. An "extra-large" is sixty to sixty-five inches. A "large" is fifty-five to sixty inches, and the medium and small grades are below that. Each five-inch increment in size brings a different price. Every trapper has these numbers permanently etched in his brain.

We would all like to catch only blankets and supers, which is the size of the older, mature adults. I always try to catch them first, and then pull my traps and move on. Unfortunately, it does not always work that way. When the ice has yet to go out, these big old ones are what you usually catch first with pole sets around their cache piles.

However, once the water opens up, the large and extra-large beaver seem to want to move out on their own. They travel, I guess, because the old ones kick them out of the house and there is still a young generation in the house that will take their place. These young ones also swim around and move some distance.

As a result, when trapping in open water after ice-out, there are beaver all over the place. The large and extra-large-sized ones are mating and trying to find places where they can build a house and start families of their own. Along streams, you'll catch them in sets for otter at locations far from a live beaver pond.

I've always taken great pride in the condition of my fur. I skin, flesh and stretch my beaver with great care. I skin them clean. When I return to camp with the green hides, I place them over my knee and scrape any remaining meat and fat off them. When they have dried, I thoroughly brush them. My fur always looks better than that of most other trappers. Fur buyers usually pay a little extra for mine.

I went back to trapping immediately after the war. In the fall, I trapped mink as soon as they became prime. I trapped and snared wolves for their bounty and hides during the winter. In the spring, I trapped beaver and otter out in the Primitive Area. I started guiding fishermen at the resorts during the summer. I couldn't have been happier.

Since the early 1930s, Benny Ambrose has lived on a piece of private property on the south side of Ottertrack Lake, which is on the border west of Saganaga. Initially it was owned by Lloyd K. Johnson, the son of Charlie Johnson, the old trading post owner. At some point, Lloyd K. deeded it to Benny. Benny has done an amazing amount of work at the place. This includes hauling in good black dirt by the packsack for planting flowers and a garden. Benny is now married and is raising his family out there. In spite of our earlier difficulties, I wish only the best for him.

The only other permanent and "official" occupant in the Superior Primitive Area is Dorothy Molter who lives on an island on the west end of Knife Lake. Molter is a nurse from Chicago. In the early 1930s, she moved to Knife Lake to work for a man named

Bill Berglund, a game warden out of Ely. He had a fishing camp on a piece of private land on Knife Lake that he called "Isle of Pines." As he became older, Molter cared for him. When he died in 1948, his brother and sister deeded the place to Molter. She gets plenty of visitors in the summer, but is pretty much alone out there in the winter. It doesn't seem to bother her.

The Forest Service keeps constant pressure on Molter and Ambrose to sell. I wonder how long they can hold out in the face of threats of condemnation. Fortunately, both of them have some very influential friends.

Our daughter, Sister, married Jack Blackwell. Jack is the son of Johnny Blackwell, the previous game warden and CCC supervisor. Johnny is the son of John A. Blackwell, whom I call "Old John." He was our local newspaper publisher for many years.

Old John first came to Grand Marais from Minneapolis in 1906 to stake stone and timber claims. He'd taken time off from his newspaper job down there after learning how profitable these claims could be. He arrived on the steamer Simon Lee. It had a steel hull and had to break ice four inches thick all the way from Duluth. It was February and amazing that boats were still running. John McKinley was the head county surveyor at that time. Blackwell talked him into going out to stake the claims with him, and McKinley advised him about the best places left to claim. They snowshoed twenty miles north to East and West Twin Lakes, and Old John staked his claims in some stands of large white pine. The weather got very cold, and he came back to Grand Marais to file his claims in the land office. His trip had taken a long time, and he missed the last boat of the year back to Duluth. He checked in to the Paine Hotel until he could figure out what to do next.

Old John must have known something I don't understand. I thought there was a 160-acre maximum for stone and timber claims, and you could only file one claim. In later years, he regularly told people he filed on five forty-acre tracts of land east of the trail to the two lakes, and 164 acres between the two lakes. That equals 364 acres. He must have been able to file more than one claim. Or, perhaps he also filed claims for his wife and one of his children. If it is true, he really did get into a valuable undertaking because of the large white pine in this area. The county surveyor was with him, so the acreages are probably accurate and must have been legal.

To get home to Minneapolis, Old John hired a local Indian who had a team of malamutes and a sled. It might have been Swamper Cariboo. The Indian agreed to haul him a hundred miles to the nearest railway at Kawishiwi, near Ely, a three day trip. During one noon stop, Old John took off his boots to dry them by the fire. The malamutes ate them. The solution to this problem was to cut a wool blanket in strips and wrap his feet in them. It worked well enough to complete the trip.

Old John limped off the train in Minneapolis, none the worse, and went back to his newspaper job. He told everyone there that this country really appealed to him. It was all he could talk about. In the fall he quit his job, purchased a printing press, and returned to Grand Marais with his family. He started his own newspaper called the Grand Marais News. After fourteen months, he bought out his competitor's newspaper, the Cook County Herald, and the resultant Cook County News-Herald is still our paper today.

Old John's son, Johnny, had been a game warden. He quit after the incident where he'd been working for two weeks, not knowing that he'd been laid off. Johnny worked for the CCCs for a while. During the war years he ran a power shovel, helping build the Alaska Highway at Destruction Bay and elsewhere in the Kluane Lake region of the Yukon Territory. He later had a construction outfit in Grand Marais. Eventually, he went back into law enforcement. He became the village marshal for Grand Marais and remained in that job for many years. He carried a .38 caliber revolver and a spring-loaded, leather-padded sap. The end was filled with lead shot. He never had to use the pistol. When he encountered combative drunks, he'd just tap them once with that sap and they became cooperative. He was non-confrontational and had a low-key approach. He never had any trouble.

Johnny's son, Jack, married Sister in 1946. Jack had returned from war service with the 15th Air Force in Europe. He was a crew member on bombers and won the Distinguished Flying Cross and the Air Medal with three oak leaf clusters. He never talked about it. With his exceptional war record and his father's previous service as a game warden, he had no trouble getting hired as a Minnesota game warden.

They assigned him to Ely. He never talked about this either, but a story is told that one day someone fired a shot that struck a tree near his head. It was a warning shot, and he heeded it. He quit and returned to Grand Marais. He became a commercial fisherman on Lake Superior for a time, and then became a log truck driver and heavy equipment operator. Jack and Sister have three children; Jacky, Mary, and Billy.

Our oldest daughter, Betty, married a man named Calvin. They had two children, Roxy and John. Betty divorced Calvin, and later married Vernon Soderlund from Hovland. He is a close friend of Clyde Wishcop, the son of my old trapping partner, Alex Wishcop. Betty and Vernon have two children, named Rob and Barbara. Vernon is a fine stone mason. The family moved to Denver for his work.

Jo was an excellent grandmother. She helped our two daughters when their children were born, and she takes care of them whenever she can. She bakes them fudge and makes their birthday cakes. They all call her "Gammie," and they call me "Gampie." They are around our house a lot.

My father, Aleck, died in 1947, at the age of ninety-four. My mother, Hannah, died in 1928. She was seventy-nine. Six years after my mother died, my father had moved to Clearwater to be with Charlie and Petra. He lived in one of their small cabins at the resort until his death. Charlie took great care of our father right up until the end.

The new prosperity after World War II, coupled with the large number of pilots returning, led to a big increase in flying. We had a lot of airplanes back in the Primitive Area for a few years. Small resorts sprang up on isolated pieces of private land. Guests were flown in to these resorts, which led to hard feelings with other visitors who paddled and portaged for days to reach some of these areas.

Probably the most flamboyant and famous of all the early pilots was Dusty Rhoades. He flew from Sody's Point on Lake Vermillion. He also owned a movie theatre in Virginia, Minnesota, and had a home there. They said he was a very good and capable bush pilot. I don't have any first-hand knowledge, because I never flew with him. Hoot Hautala was my pilot. Like Hoot, Dusty was rumored to fly illegal trappers into the Superior Primitive Area and the Quetico Provincial Park. He was also rumored to fly liquor from Campbell's Resort on Lac La Croix Lake in Canada to the United States during Prohibition. The booze was legal in Canada. Dusty also became the first floatplane pilot hired by the Forest Service, and he flew for them for a short time.

In 1927, Charles Lindbergh flew the Spirit of St. Louis across the Atlantic Ocean to Paris. It was big news, and everyone talked about it. A wealthy mining man in Eveleth, named Kingston, had to have one. He purchased a Ryan B-1 plane just like Lindbergh's and named it the Spirit of St. Louis County. He bought floats and skis for the plane and hired Dusty to fly it. During the winter and spring, Kingston took long, extended vacations to the south and west. He'd leave the plane with Dusty, giving him permission to use it. One of the first things Dusty did was to invite the new Game and Fish Commissioner from St. Paul to Ely for a flight over the massive game refuge. Rhoades tried to talk him into hiring him and the airplane for state wildlife patrol. The commissioner didn't go for it.

Kingston went into partnership with Dusty and they called their company Kingston-Rhoades Airways. Dusty made great use of the plane and he became widely known. He flew illegal trappers and legal fishermen into the Superior Primitive Area. The illegal trapping out of Ely got more and more publicity. A few of the trappers became bold and cocky. Someone even "bombed" the Game and Fish cabin headquarters in Winton with beaver carcasses dropped from an airplane. Dusty was the chief suspect. I hated hearing these things, because I thought it would just result in more law enforcement.

Dusty Rhoades bought a small piece of land somewhere north of Lake Vermillion and announced he was going into the beaver farming business. His plan was to buy illegal beaver hides directly from trappers and market them as coming from his farm. This became a big business for him.

As Rhoades's publicity mounted, so did the efforts to catch him. Both the Minnesota and Ontario governments were determined to get him. He barely escaped being caught by two game wardens on snowshoes on Little Saganaga. He and a trapper got away in the plane, but they had to abandon two packsacks and a gunnysack full of beaver hides. I didn't think it was very smart to land on that particular lake with a game warden cabin located on it.

Another time, an elaborate undercover operation took place in Virginia. It involved a big fur buyer from Minneapolis who was supposed to be cooperating with the state. (I'm not so sure about that.) The buyer arranged to purchase over three hundred beaver hides from Rhoades. The deal was to take place at Dusty's home. A raiding party of eight game wardens waited nearby with a search warrant. They were led by my old supervisor, Joe Brickner, who was now the chief warden at Hibbing. Somehow, the buyer gave the signal for the raiding party to come in at the wrong time. Only fifty-five beaver were found in the house. Three hundred twenty-eight beaver hides had already been measured, graded, sorted, and counted. They were loaded in the buyer's car out back. A warden had left his post in the back. In all the confusion, Dusty snuck out the back door and disappeared with the buyer's car. When the car was found a few days later, the beaver hides were missing. Using the old average of $30 apiece, this was close to $10,000 in fur, which is a lot of money, especially in those days.

When they found him, Rhoades was arrested and charged in district court in Virginia with illegal possession of beaver. I don't think the fur buyer was ever charged with anything. Dusty demanded a jury trial. At the trial, he claimed the beaver all came from his beaver farm. The state presented expert testimony, stating this was physically and biologically impossible. The jury found him not guilty. It was identical to situation I had experienced in Grand Marais. I felt terrible for the wardens, but it demonstrated, once again, the total lack of support in northern Minnesota for the absurd game refuge regulations.

The Canadians were determined to get Rhoades. In an undercover operation at Campbell's Resort near the Lac La Croix Indian village, he attempted to take off with a member of the Royal Canadian Mounted Police standing on one pontoon and a Canadian customs officer on the other. They ordered him to stop. When Rhoades kept his engine at full power, the Mountie drew his revolver, smashed open the side window, leveled his pistol at Rhoades's head, and ordered him to cut the engine. It was a good thing Dusty stopped. I think that Mountie would have shot him in a heartbeat. Dusty must have thought so, too. He was arrested, taken into custody, and transported by water and land, first to Fort Frances, and then to Winnipeg. He got out of jail by paying a substantial fine. The airplane was pulled up on shore and impounded at Campbell's Resort. It took months for Dusty and the mining man to get it back. They had to go back to Winnipeg and pay a $1200 fine. The Canadians don't fool around with things like this.

Walter Caribou was living at Lac La Croix village, next to Campbell's, at this time. Walter told me Dusty returned for the plane during December, after the lake had frozen up. He warmed up the engine and got Campbell's people and Indian people from the village to help push it out on the ice. There was very little snow, and he successfully took off, dragging the pontoons over the ice and snow. He flew the plane down to Eveleth where he must have had to land the plane on ice as well.

Between all the upset canoeists and the negative publicity about flying illegal trappers, it had to come to an end. And it did. First, congress passed the Thye-Blatnik Act of 1948 that required the Forest Service to acquire the private lands by either purchase or condemnation. This resulted in bitter hatred of the Forest Service from some of our local people who refused to sell their private land. Their land was therefore condemned and taken from them, although they were paid what was determined to be fair market value.

President Truman signed an Executive Order in 1949 prohibiting airplanes from flying below four thousand feet mean sea level. It went into effect in 1952. That ended the low-level airplane flying, except for firefighting, law enforcement, search and rescue, administrative use, and fish stocking. There were a number of commercial airplane operations scattered around the edge of the Primitive Area that catered to people who wanted to fly into the Primitive Area. They were put out of business.

At Ely, it marked the end of flying for Hoot Hautala. He gave up his business, although his two sons are still flying. Dusty Rhoades was never seen again. Some people say the air ban drove him out, and others say he was gone long before that because of all his legal troubles and close encounters with the law. Regardless, Dusty got out while the getting was good, and while he still had substantial profits.

On the Gunflint Trail, Emerson Morris had to shut down his flying business at Poplar Lake and move to Grand Marais, where he became a deputy sheriff and then county sheriff. At Sea Gull Lake, Williard Waters had to shut down Waters Airways. Williard stayed there and did some trapping himself. He kept a Piper Cub on floats at Sea Gull for many more years. He made his plane available for emergencies in the Primitive Area, and performed some valuable search and rescue flights.

The Thye-Blatnik Act and the Presidential Air Ban brought wilderness conditions back to the areas in the Primitive Area that were being developed. But it was heavy-hammer remedy, and it was very hard on some of our local people who are still not over it. There may have been no other way. I understand why it had to be done, and am grateful it happened.

In the fall of 1949, I was trapping mink with Buck Smith along the headwaters of the North Brule River. One day we witnessed something remarkable. We were quietly paddling along, very close to the shoreline on Vista Lake. A rabbit came running out of the woods and came down to the edge of the lake. Right behind it came a fisher in hot pursuit. The fisher maneuvered the rabbit up against the lake shore. It was either swim or head back into the woods for the rabbit. It darted back for the woods, and the fisher nailed it. This is the way life works in nature. It all happened right in front of us. It was a good demonstration of what I already knew. That is, if you want to see animals from a canoe, be quiet and stay as close to the shoreline as possible. Otherwise, they will see you, and avoid you if they can.

A week or so later, Buck learned that he had a construction job with Ed Thoresen. He left to take it, and is still working for Ed. Ed Thoresen Construction Company has become the largest road builder in the county.

With our daughters married, and children around, Jo and I had settled in to a routine where I trapped and guided for a living. Jo was always involved with our grandchildren and continued to babysit for other families around town for extra money.

11

The 1950s

I continued to trap mink in the fall and beaver in the spring out in the Primitive Area. In the summer, I guided fishermen at Carl Brandt's Wilderness Retreat Resort on McFarland Lake or at Jean Raiken's Sawbill Lodge. In my spare time, I trapped and snared timber wolves for their bounty, which was now up to $35. I also hunted birds and deer.

The only close call I ever had with an animal was a moose. It happened during the spring, and it was a cow with her calf. I got too close to them, and that cow came after me lickety-split. She chased me round and round a small spruce tree, while trying to kick me with her front feet. I had my axe in my hand, but that was it. I swung at her a few times as I ran around that tree and tried to keep it between us. Eventually she gave up. I sure never hurt her.

I learned to pay attention to the mountain ash trees. The Indians believe a heavy berry crop in the fall means a hard winter will follow. The mountain ash is also an important tree for wildlife. When you see fresh broken branches on a tree in the fall it means a bear has been up there pulling off the branches to get at the berries. Many of the berries remain on the tree over winter and birds like them. By spring, the berries can ferment and partridge will eat them. I have seen drunken partridges flying around, banging into things. It is quite a sight.

Whenever I shoot a duck, I remove its guts and bring it home that way. If I'm living out in the woods, I skin and fry it, but they taste better baked at home. I have never had to pluck feathers from my ducks. Jo's Indian mother, Jane, taught her that that is the woman of the house's job. I never even had to ask. I am very fortunate.

I also like to hunt partridge and waterfowl with my dog. I tie my own trout flies from deer hair and supplies ordered out of the Herter's catalogue. I was busy with all of this.

On a trapping trip northeast of Alice Lake, I had some bad luck, which actually turned to good luck. I struck a match to light my pipe. The match tip broke and the burning end flew into my big box of kitchen matches. They instantly caught fire. I got them outside without anything else catching on fire, but now my match supply was very low. I had matches left in my two Marble waterproof match containers, but that was it. I had to be very frugal in using them. I was worried how long they would last. A few days later, I discovered a coffee can turned upside down at a lakeshore campsite. Inside, I found .22 shells and matches. My problem was over. I learned a lesson I still follow. Today, I make sure I have at least two separate supplies of matches in my camps.

Another time, I was trapping north of the Big Bend country. You don't hear the Mahlberg Lake area referred to as the Big Bend country much anymore. Old-timers so named it because of the great distance water has to flow from its west end all the way down the lake to the east, around the corner, and then all the way back on what is the headwaters of the North Kawishiwi River. It's only a 25-rod portage from the west end of the lake over to the river. However, a cup of water on the Mahlberg Lake side has to flow over eight miles to get to the river on the other side of the short portage.

On this trip, my back completely went out on me. I lay flat in camp for two days, and could not get back trapping for a week. Fortunately, I had plenty of firewood cut and split in advance. Not having to leave camp to find and cut wood helped me recover more quickly. You never know what might happen to you. Be prepared.

A disease called tularemia swept through our beaver country during the winter of 1952. It killed beaver indiscriminately. Tens of thousands, if not more, died. There had been an overpopulation of beaver and this was nature's way of thinning them out. It was another indication of the folly of the massive game refuge in the Primitive Area. The beaver population came back, thankfully.

In 1952, the DNR completely opened the large game refuge in the Superior Primitive Area to beaver trapping. Maybe it was the tularemia outbreak that finally did it. The Division of Game and Fish would later say, "It is now obvious that posting and maintaining such large areas in the canoe country is unnecessary, since hunters reach only a small part of them." They also said, "We have learned through sad experience, surveys, and management methods that complete protection is not the answer. Complete protection results in over-browsed big game range, disease, starvation, and law enforcement problems … Game populations on refuge areas should be utilized if surpluses exist."

Finally, we trappers and the northern Minnesota public were shown to be right. It was bittersweet. Since 1909 we had been legally prohibited from making our living. If the Division of Game and Fish thought they had gone through a "sad experience," imagine what it had been like for us. Hundreds of us had been arrested and fined. We always lived in fear of being discovered. We were barely able to eke out a living and our families had suffered greatly. This change was monumental. I wish the state would have come out with an apology, but that wasn't going to happen. Those written comments were all we ever got.

In the mid-1950s, the Erie Mining Company came into our lives. Erie Mining decided to develop a new open-pit iron ore mine. It was to produce concentrated taconite pellets for shipment by railroad to the shore of Lake Superior. This was a huge undertaking, with many jobs created, both during construction, and after the plant was operational. Erie Mining built the new town of Hoyt Lakes to house their workers near Aurora, twenty-five miles south of Ely. On the other end, they built the much smaller town of Taconite Harbor on the shore of Lake Superior. Workers there unload taconite into boats and operate a coal-fired power plant, which produces electricity for operations back in Hoyt Lakes. A railroad and a big high voltage power line were built between the two locations. Ore boats on the Great Lakes haul the taconite to steel mills near Cleveland, and return with a load of coal for the power plant.

These were good, high-paying construction jobs. The company advertised for local workers. I decided to apply for a job cutting lines through the woods for their surveyors. People thought I was too old for that kind of hard, physical work, but I have always been in good shape. The company called me in for an interview. I think what made the difference in getting hired was my experience doing the same kind of work for the International Boundary Commission many years earlier.

They took a chance hiring me, and I made sure they never regretted it. I worked as hard, or harder, than any of the younger guys. I was experienced with the work and knew what to do without being asked. I don't drink or party, so I was always on the job, focused and ready to produce. For me, the work lasted over a year. The pay was the most I have ever earned. I still pull out some of the old check stubs and look at them longingly. Following the job with Erie Mining, I went back to my pattern of trapping and guiding. I continued to hunt and fish whenever I could. My dry flies got better and trout fishing was good.

Sister's husband, Jack, was hired to operate heavy equipment for the construction of the railroad and power line. When construction was finished, he went on to work for Erie Mining at Taconite Harbor, using a crane to unload coal from the boats and keep the power plant fed.

As a child, Sister had developed a limp in her right leg. It got worse. By the time she was thirteen years old, doctors decided she needed an operation on the bone in that leg. Over the years, she required nine more. After one of them, the doctors confided to Jo and me that it was tuberculosis in her bone. She had probably contracted it from drinking unpasteurized milk on a visit to my family's farm back in Milaca. Based on the doctor's advice, for a long time we didn't tell Sister that she had tuberculosis.

Sister was a very brave young woman to endure the pain from all those operations. After she was married and had three children she learned the truth. By then, doctors recommended she check in to the Nopeming Sanatorium located south of Duluth. Following treatments there, and two more years taking fifty pills each day, she is now free from TB. However, her right leg is one inch shorter than her left one. Fortunately, none of her children contracted the disease.

One fall, I was mink trapping west of Gabimichigami. In contrast to beaver trapping, where all you need for bait is a green popple stick, it is difficult to obtain good bait for mink. If you are trapping near any of the North Shore fishermen you can always get fresh herring guts, which mink really like early in the season. But that option is not available when you're living far out in the woods.

I needed to be creative. I always keep a minnow trap at my cabins that I use to catch minnows for bait, for both mink and my fishing lines. When it is not catching minnows, I use the minnow trap to catch mice in the cabin. I also have some ice fishing lines I can tie to shore. I may have even used a small piece of net to catch northerns.

The weather got cold. One day, I set three traps along a stream coming in to a lake. I made traditional cubby sets. In the first two cubbies, I used fish for bait. In the last cubby, I used a fresh red squirrel that I shot out of a spruce tree nearby. Indians know that mink hate red squirrels. The squirrels chatter overhead and scold the mink all the time.

Three days later, I returned. There was a fresh snow. I quickly spotted tracks where a big mink had come out of the lake and started traveling upstream toward my traps. At the first set he investigated from twenty feet away, but went right past it. The same thing happened at the second set. When he came to the third set with the red squirrel, he didn't hesitate, and dove right into the cubby. I had him. He was a beautiful big male, already drowned from the weight of the trap in the running water.

This is a good example of what I have learned about the eating habits of mink. They change from fish to meat when it gets cold. I know some trappers will use a lure for mink, but I have no experience with this method.

I didn't always trap alone. Some years I had partners. I talked previously about Harry Hummitch, Alex Wishcop, and Buck Smith. Some of the others were Clifford Samuelson, Bud Lindzy, and Axel

Berglund. At times, Axel would take offense at the slightest little thing and not talk to me for days. Most times, I would not even know what I had done to offend him. In spite of this, we managed to make it work, and he was a good trapper.

Keeping track of the days while trapping can be a problem. After thirty days or more, it's impossible to remember what day it is, or how many have gone by. Some trappers bring a calendar and cross off each day. Others will hang their calendar on the wall and drive a small nail through each day. But you have to remember to do it, and then you wonder, "have I marked my calendar today?" What I do, when I am alone, is bring a fresh box of fifty cigars. I treat myself to one each night. I look forward to this and never have to remember if I've done it. To determine how much time has elapsed, I simply count the remaining cigars.

The US Air Force built a radar site at a location north of the small town of Finland. It is on Highway 1, between the North Shore and Ely. The radar was part of a secondary warning system below the Distant Early Warning (DEW) Line in Canada. It didn't last very long. Out in the Primitive Area, I started to come across areas of aluminum chaff on the ground. There were quite a few of them. I think they were part of testing for the new radar site. After a couple of years, they disintegrated and disappeared. I no longer see them.

Betty's children were in Denver, but Sister's were here. I started taking her oldest son, Jacky, with me when he was ten or eleven years old. First, it was day trips fishing and hunting. Later, we went out overnight on trips to my cabins in the Primitive Area or to Harry Hummitch's old cabin on Crocodile. By that time, Jacky was also hunting and trapping with his father and Johnny, his other grandfather. Sister's daughter, Mary, has become a fine pianist. Billy is still a youngster. Who knows where life will take them?

I continued to live out in the Primitive Area during the fall and spring. I know Sister's children were always concerned their Gampie would not be home in time for Thanksgiving. Most years I made it with a few days to spare.

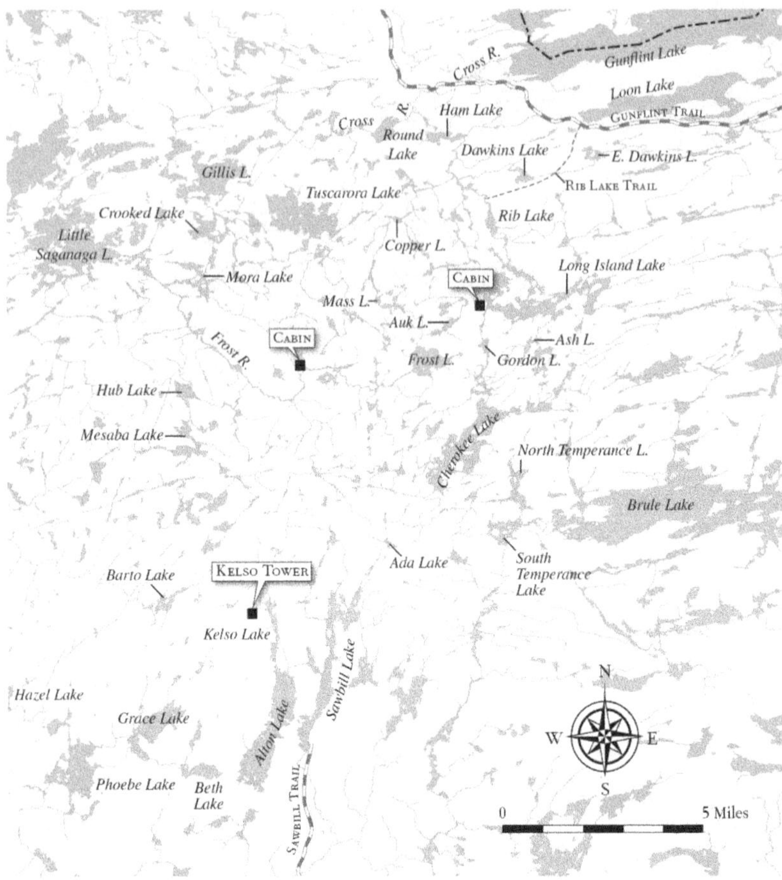
Cross R.
Gunflint Lake
Loon Lake
Cross R.
Ham Lake
GUNFLINT TRAIL
Round Lake
Dawkins Lake
E. Dawkins L.
Gillis L.
Tuscarora Lake
RIB LAKE TRAIL
Rib Lake
Crooked Lake
Little Saganaga L.
Copper L.
Long Island Lake
Mora Lake
CABIN
Mass L.
Auk L.
Frost R.
CABIN
Ash L.
Frost L.
Gordon L.
Hub Lake
Mesaba Lake
Cherokee Lake
North Temperance L.
Brule Lake
Barto Lake
KELSO TOWER
Ada Lake
South Temperance Lake
Kelso Lake
Sawbill Lake
Hazel Lake
Grace Lake
Alton Lake
N
W E
S
Phoebe Lake
Beth Lake
SAWBILL TRAIL
0
5 Miles

12

My Last Trip with Charlie

My brother, Charlie, and I had grown apart over the years. It was bound to happen. He and Petra have their lives and friends there at Clearwater and elsewhere on the Gunflint Trail. Their ten children are grown and married. Most of them still live in the area, and now there are many grandchildren with whom they are occupied. In addition, Charlie never learned to drive. He walks, runs a boat, paddles a canoe, or depends on others to drive him where he wants to go.

Jo and I still live in Grand Marais. Local telephone service to Clearwater has become good. Jo and Petra are good friends, and talk regularly.

It was the winter of 1962. I had been trying to snare wolves south of Clearwater, down by Caribou Lake. One day, after checking my snares, I was seated with Charlie and Petra at their kitchen table, looking out over the lake. I talked about last fall's mink trapping trip. I could tell Charlie was really interested. I had been using my cabin on the west end of Long Island. I also have another cabin a day's travel farther west on the Frost River.

I said, "Charlie, if you feel up to it, why don't you come beaver trapping with me this spring?"

"I'll think about it," was all he said.

"Fine. I have all the traps, most of the food and gear, and almost everything we need already out there. If you decide to come, you need to limit yourself to one pack of no more than forty pounds, including your sleeping bag. I'll bring some more food and whatever else we'll need."

In a day or two, Petra reported to Jo that Charlie wanted to come. By this time, he was seventy-two and I was sixty-two. We never talk about our ages. We just do what we have always done,

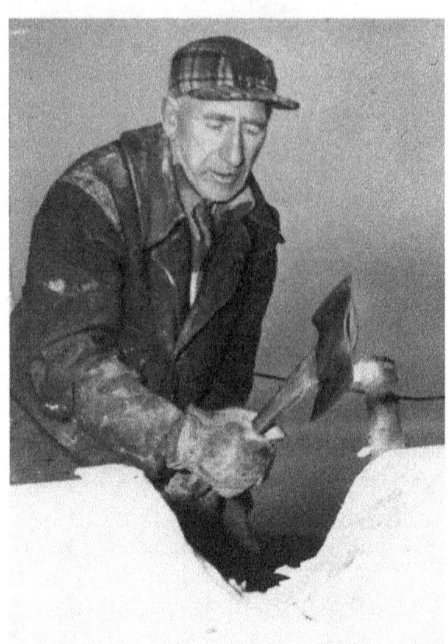

Charlie Boostrom building a log cabin. He is reported to have built over 100 log cabins in Cook County. Cook County Historical Society

even if we have a few more aches and pains.

The old game refuge is finally gone, and there was a legal beaver season that year. It went from mid-March until the first of May. Game wardens no longer run patrols on foot through the deep part of the Superior Primitive Area. Many of their cabins are also gone, and so are most of the old-time wardens. There aren't many of us trappers left that still go out there, either.

The limit that year was ten beaver apiece, but there is a way around that if you buy licenses for relatives and friends. Being the only trappers in such a vast area, we sure weren't going to hurt them by catching more than ten. Cabins have long been illegal in the National Forest Primitive Area, but mine were carefully hidden. There was less risk from the law now than there had been in the old days.

I went up to Clearwater a couple more times before we were due to depart the last week of March. There was about three feet of snow on the ground, which was normal for this time of the year. We finalized our plans, and made arrangements with a trusted neighbor named Oscar to drive us farther up the Gunflint Trail to the Rib Lake Trail.

We also instructed Oscar when to come back to get us. This meant driving my car up to the Cross River on the side road to Round Lake on a specific date during the first week of May. If we weren't there, we asked him to do the same thing late every afternoon until we showed up.

The trip would be old hat for Charlie and me. Neither of us thought there would be any problems we couldn't handle. We were comfortable with each other, and could pretty well predict what the other would do in any given situation.

The day to leave came quickly. I drove up to Clearwater the night before, and we left early in the morning in the dark. Oscar drove us up to the Rib Lake Trail. There were no tracks in the snow. I had him go a little farther, where some trees and brush came closer to the road. We parked, unloaded our snowshoes and our two packs. I lifted Charlie's and sure enough, it was no more than forty pounds. Mine was closer to fifty.

In order to leave less of an obvious trail, we struggled on foot through the snow bank left by the plow. We didn't put on our snow-shoes until we were well in the woods. We always did things like this to keep people from spotting our snowshoe tracks and wondering who made them, where we were going, and what we were up to.

I broke trail and Charlie kept up. So far, this was looking like a good start to our trip. In three miles, we came to Rib Lake. Breaking trail while wearing a fifty-pound pack was hard work, but I could tell we were going to make it to Long Island before dark. Charlie was still doing fine.

The old Rib Lake Trail comes out on the north end of the lake. From here, the canoe route goes to Long Island. It follows Rib Lake south for about two miles, then continues upstream on the Cross River to a couple of other lakes before coming to Long Island.

Where the river comes in at the south end of Rib Lake, there is always thin ice and some open water. There's a good chance you'll break through and at least get your feet wet. After almost fifty years around there, I have learned the hard way to keep away from that place in the winter.

There is a good-sized bay at the southwest end of the lake, and I led us down to it. From here, there is a series of beaver ponds and a small lake leading down to the west end of Long Island. We followed this route and arrived on the lake by mid-afternoon. It was only a mile or so farther to my cabin. Charlie was still keeping up on the trail I was breaking, but both of us were taking longer, and more frequent, rest stops.

We continued down to the west end of the lake and climbed up the steep shoreline to my hidden cabin. Everything appeared just as I had left it a couple of months earlier when I had snowshoed out there to deliver food to the cabin. As far as I could tell, nothing had been disturbed, and there was no sign of anyone being around.

I grabbed some birch bark and dry kindling I always keep inside, and fired up the Airtight stove. In no time at all, the small cabin was warm and toasty. We carried in our packs. Charlie dug into his and brought out his down sleeping bag. I got mine out from the five-gallon lard can that I use to keep it away from mice.

I got a pretty good look at what was left in Charlie's pack, and I swear it was mostly plug tobacco! There might have been a change of underwear and a couple pair of wool socks, but that was it.

Before it got dark, there were two things outside I needed to check on. I grabbed a small container of oil and went out back. I had left my 12 gauge Winchester Model 12 shotgun in a big hollow birch tree, and I went there first. I reached up into the tree above the rotten opening and sure enough, there it was, dry and rust-free. I rubbed some oil on its metal surface and worked the oil inside on the moving parts. I put the gun back in its storage place in the tree.

Then, I went farther back to check where I had hidden Charlie's canoe. It's a Grumman fifteen-foot lightweight with a nice custom yoke I built. It has a noticeable kink in the bow caused by flying off a car on a duck hunting trip Charlie had taken to Canada. I'd used the canoe last fall trapping mink, but now we would need it for beaver. I dug it out of the snow and determined it was still fine.

I went back to the cabin and gave a report to Charlie. While I was gone, he had found everything he needed and had already started supper, which was going to be bannock and beans. We talked while we waited for the meal to cook.

"Charlie, I know you're tired and we've come a good distance today, but if you're up to it, I'd like to leave first thing in the morning for my cabin down on the Frost River. There are many more beaver in that country and I think that's where we need to be this year."

"Fine by me," was all he said.

"I'll come back for the canoe as the country opens up. We should be able to make the same kind of time going down there tomorrow that we made today."

We ate supper, lit a candle for a short time, and went to bed. The days are much longer when beaver trapping in the spring than they are in the fall mink trapping, so you don't need a candle or lantern as much during the spring.

In the morning, we were both up early. Again, Charlie did the cooking. He prepared two plates of pancakes, and we ate them quickly. He made extra pancakes for lunch. I put my sleeping bag back in its storage container, and we packed up. I made certain there was a new supply of birch bark and kindling near the stove. This is a basic safety precaution you must follow. You, or someone else, might come back cold, wet, and miserable and need to get a fire started quickly. It could save your life.

We closed the place up and put on our snowshoes. This time, instead of going down to the lake, I led off through the woods in a straight westerly direction. Within a short distance, the vegetation changed dramatically, and we entered the country of the 1936 burn. It had been a big fire. The young popple and birch coming back are ideal beaver food, and the country is easy to walk through. There are also many partridge and quite a few moose in this second growth forest.

My route took us across Auke Lake, north of Frost Lake, and down some small lakes, beaver ponds, and streams to the Frost River which flows west to Little Sag. From here, we followed the river down to my cabin, which is on the north side of the river. It is in another hidden location, and we walked up to it.

Again, everything appeared fine, but the normally quiet Charlie had something to say. "God almighty, Alec! Why in the world would you ever build a cabin under a big boulder that looks ready to fall on it?"

The cabin was next to a rock ledge, and perched on top of the ledge is a narrow, top-heavy rock about four feet tall. I said, "Charlie, that rock has been here since the last glacier left it, and it will still be here when the next one comes along."

He just shook his head. We went inside, but I knew he thought I was nuts. He would always be worried staying here. It really is an ideal spot to hide a cabin, there between the rock ledge and a spruce swamp the fire had gone around.

We quickly settled in to a routine, and it was a good one. Charlie did all the cooking. I got a kick out of introducing him to a new food that has come along in recent years that is ideal for trappers like us. Instant mashed potato flakes are light to carry and quick to prepare.

We also ate a lot of bannock. Sometimes Charlie would lightly fry it on top of the stove, and sometimes he would bake it and let it brown, up close to the side of the stove. Sometimes he did both. The basic recipe for bannock is easy to remember; 1:1:1. That is, one cup of flour, one teaspoon of baking powder and one pinch of salt. You mix the three ingredients and then add water slowly and knead it thoroughly into a doughy consistency. Sometimes Charlie would add raisins or a little brown sugar for variety. I've also seen him wrap the dough around a green stick in a series of spirals and bake it outside beside an open fire. Bannock has been around forever, and is great for trappers. I've been eating it on my traplines my entire life.

Charlie gathered all the firewood. He mended our gear, kept up the camp, and sewed the beaver on hoops when I started catching them. I was free to use all my accumulated years of experience and high energy to just trap and catch beaver. Charlie took care of drying the fur, and everything else back in camp. We were highly efficient, and the beaver hides started piling up.

One late afternoon, I came in and looked closely at Charlie. He didn't seem right. I could tell something was wrong.

"Are you feeling OK?" I asked him.

He didn't want to tell me, but said "No, I'm all bound up. I've tried birch bark tea and every other woods remedy that I know, but nothing's worked."

"How long has it been since you've shit?"

"Oh, about a week."

I thought for a while. This could turn into a serious emergency if we didn't get him treated soon.

"I'll leave for Sawbill Lake early in the morning. The guard station will not be occupied this early in the year. With luck, I'll find Jean Raiken at home and she'll have something you can use. I know Frank and Mary Alice Hansen won't be up at their canoe outfitters yet. So, if the Raiken's aren't home, I may have to find a ride all the way to Tofte. I could be gone overnight."

"I'm really sorry to cause you all this trouble, Alec."

"You'd do the same thing for me, Brother."

We ate supper. Charlie cooked up a good supply of pancakes and beaver meat for me to carry tomorrow. We turned in early.

I was up by three o'clock and out of there on my snowshoes shortly after. I could see well enough to travel. There was a heavy crust on the snow that I knew would last at least until noon.

I kept my speed up. All I carried on my back was a light pack with a dry pair of wool socks in case my feet got wet and the food Charlie had prepared. I carried my single-bit axe in my hand.

The ice had raised on some of the lakes. On these, I could take off my snowshoes and walk on foot. I just ate up the miles. I had to be sure not to get careless, especially where I crossed the upper Cherokee River.

Around daylight, I came out on the north end of Sawbill. From there, it was a six-mile walk on the raised ice down to the resort on the south end.

I was in luck. Jean and her husband, Dick, were eating breakfast when I came into their yard. Their dog barked, and they spotted me.

Jean said "Alec, what are you doing coming off the lake at this time of the day? Is something wrong?"

I tried to delicately explain about Charlie, but gave up and bluntly asked if they had any laxatives I could have. Again my luck was good, because they did. They willingly let me have their supply. I offered to pay, but they wouldn't hear of it.

Jean was a county commissioner and had been the representative for the west end of the county since the mid-1950s. Dick works for the Forest Service in the summer, maintaining their campgrounds on the upper Sawbill Trail.

They both knew to keep their mouths shut. They own their resort, but the land it is located on is under permit from the Forest Service. It would never go well for them if the Forest Service, or the game wardens, found out about them helping Charlie and me. Nor would it go well for us if the wrong person heard about it. No one ever did.

I was gone within twenty minutes of arriving. My trip back also went well. I beat the afternoon thawing temperatures and the crust held up for me all the way back.

Charlie was busy working on a hide when I came in.

"Here's a present from Jean and Dick for you," was all I said as I handed him the package.

I won't go into details, but I will tell you by nighttime Charlie was all smiles. I was happy too. We had avoided a major disaster and could now get back to trapping beaver. The season went on, and the river opened up. I brought the canoe down from Long Island. Our success was fantastic.

Near the end, Charlie said, "That's it Alec. We have enough. Let's quit while we're ahead."

"No way," I responded. "I've had too many years with small catches and I'll be darned if I quit now when things are going so well." That quieted him, but I knew how he felt.

By season's end we had 120 beaver! Charlie had done all the cooking, gathered the dry firewood from a farther and farther distance, took care of all the fur, and in his spare time, managed to catch twenty-three beaver using the canoe on the river near the cabin. He was incredible.

I made a monster bale of ninety beaver hides and put them in my special packsack with the extra twelve-inch sidewalls sewn in. It was heavy, but I could carry it. The other thirty went into Charlie's pack. He said he could handle it.

Early the next morning, we took off in the canoe and paddled our way upstream, following the river and portages to Frost Lake. The ground was bare, but most of the lake was still frozen solid. We kept our packs in the canoe and pulled it on the raised ice along the south shore to the two portages, and over to Gordon. From Gordon, it was open water down to Long Island. That big lake was still frozen, and we made it safely over the ice to my cabin.

We spent the night at the cabin, and were off pulling the canoe on the ice again the next morning. After Long Island, everything was wide open. We paddled downstream along the lakes and river, and carried our heavy packs over the portages. We came to Rib Lake, and continued on down the Cross River. The last lake is Ham Lake and then it's two short portages to the road. We never met anyone, but out of caution, we held up at the last portage before the canoe landing.

I walked through the woods down to the road. Charlie stayed behind to watch our valuable cargo. There was no one lurking about, and I stayed hidden in the woods.

Before long, Oscar showed up in the car. I came out of the woods and explained he should drive off and return one hour later. He left, and I went back for Charlie.

We hid the canoe in the woods so it wouldn't appear obvious to anyone we might meet on the road that we were coming off the water. We loaded our fur in the car, and Oscar drove us down to Clearwater. It was an uneventful ride. I came back alone the next day and retrieved the canoe.

Ted, the fur buyer from the Hudson's Bay Company in Thunder Bay, bought our fur that year and gave us a good cash price. We were happy with the amount, and split it fifty-fifty. Jo and Petra were happy too, and there was a little extra that summer for all of us.

It was a great ending to a great season. All that remained was to retrieve Charlie's down sleeping bag and both our snowshoes from the Frost River cabin. I also wanted to bring my precious shotgun home.

Later that month, Charlie and I left the Cross River landing in his trusty Grumman canoe and started a leisurely four-day trip.

The country was just as beautiful as it had been when we first saw it many years earlier. Neither of us knew how many more years we would be able to do this, and we enjoyed it immensely. We carried provisions to restock the cabins, and we paddled down to the Long Island cabin, over to the Frost River cabin, and then repeated the trip in reverse. Nothing unusual happened, except for something at Ham Lake on the return.

We came upon a campsite occupied by some tourists, obviously from somewhere far away. Our snowshoes and shotgun were plainly visible in our canoe, and we were a pair of grizzled-looking old-timers. They just stared at us. Before anyone could say anything, Charlie spoke to me in a voice they could all plainly hear.

"Well, Alec. It's been a tough winter, but I think we're going to make it." Out came the tourists' cameras, but Charlie wouldn't let us stop. Imagine the story those people told when they returned home.

That's the way my brother is. Normally soft-spoken and modest, he has developed a wicked sense of humor, which he delights in using on people he thinks will believe him. I love him dearly.

13

My Dogs

I've always been good with animals. I'm gentle with them, and we bond quickly. They seem to understand me, and something positive usually happens between us. It's hard to explain. It has always been this way for me, even back on the farm.

When I was hired for the border survey job, I was fortunate to be able to observe many different dog teams, and many different dog team owners. I got to see them work with their dogs. I formed strong opinions about which techniques worked and which ones didn't.

This first contact with so many different dog teams was invaluable. Some dog team drivers had to beat or whip their dogs to get them to obey. Others seemed to get by with only simple voice commands.

I kept my opinions to myself. Soon, I found myself working full-time in the winter, helping with the dog teams. I cooked their food, and fed and watered them. I harnessed them and loaded their sleds. I gave each dog special attention. In time, the owners let me drive them.

I came to realize that dogs are all different. They have different personalities, and they do not all act the same. In this respect, they are no different than people. But, not all people understand this.

By the end of the border survey project I was an experienced dog team driver. I didn't have my own team yet, but I could handle a dog team as well as anyone. When I came back to Clearwater, I shared some of this with Charlie. Soon, we were partners with a dog team. Because of all the construction projects with log cabins Charlie needed to build, plus being available to help Petra with their growing number of children, taking care of the dogs and working them was my responsibility. I loved it.

As far as I know, my record of running a dog team from Clearwater to Grand Marais down the Gunflint Trail still stands. It is three hours and twenty minutes over the thirty-two miles of hilly terrain.

When I left Clearwater to get married, I missed my sled dogs. I got my next dog soon after Betty was born. It was an Airedale. He was accidently poisoned after eating something he was not supposed to. I never found out how it happened, even though I tried. This lesson taught me to be very careful with my dogs around town. I had them stay close to our house and not roam.

I hunt partridge and ducks whenever I can. It is important for a hunting dog to have a "soft mouth." They should retrieve birds gently, and not chew them and break their bones. It is important to spend a lot of time training a dog to understand this.

I use a small canvas sack stuffed with straw as they learn to retrieve. I tell them not to chew it and repeat the exercise over and over. It works for us. When they move on to retrieving partridge and ducks, they have a soft mouth and are gentle with the birds.

Charlie had a big retriever named Babe. With everything going on at Clearwater, he never had enough time to work with the dog. She was big and she was rough. Babe developed a very hard mouth.

One time, Charlie had shot a couple of partridge. Babe was with him and brought them back. The birds were all chewed and mangled. That was it; this called for drastic corrective action.

Charlie fed Babe out of a big wooden bowl. He drilled a number of small holes in the bowl, through which he pounded sharpened spikes. He drove them in from the outside so the sharp points protruded into her bowl. Babe had to gently eat and lick around those sharpened nails. It helped a little bit, but Babe was never a good hunting dog.

A wealthy man with the last name of Diamond decided to organize a winter Christmas show for kids. He wanted a reindeer team and a dog team in the show. Charlie ordered nine reindeer from

Alaska and I had a dog team. Someone would dress as Santa Claus and it would be a big hit with the kids.

For two seasons, we traveled to towns in Minnesota, Wisconsin, and Michigan. I took care of the dogs and got them to understand their role and participate. Charlie and another helper took care of the reindeer. It was fun. Eventually the reindeer disappeared from Clearwater during the summer. One was spotted up near Gunflint Lake. They may have been trying to migrate back home.

My best dog by far was Sally. Sally was a golden lab, and was with me for many years. She understood everything I said. Sally always wanted to help. When we traveled, Sally could lie for hours in the ice water that had accumulated in the bottom of my canoe. She never whimpered or asked me to stop. She was loyal, and trusted me in everything.

On the trapline, when I struggled to pull a pole set up through the ice, she would tug on it to help me. She'd check on my trap sets and let me know if I had caught something.

Once, a beaver managed to break the trap loose from the rock tied on to drown it. That beaver was alive, and it was mad. Undaunted, Sally jumped in to retrieve it for me. The beaver bit Sally on her nose. It was raw and sore for weeks, but finally healed with no problems.

Sally got pregnant once when we were in town. I didn't realize she was going to have puppies until we were out on a trip. This time we were mink trapping from a small cabin southwest of Sea Gull Lake. Her five puppies were born out there. She was a good mother, and took care of them in the cabin each day.

It became time to leave. The puppies' eyes were not even open and they were not weaned. We had to walk out on the Kekekabic Trail. The solution I came up with was to carry them home in an old five-gallon lard can in the back of my packsack. I placed some soft grass and moss in the bottom of the can, put them inside, and closed the lid to keep them warm.

Off we went with the puppies whining and crying for their mother. Pretty soon, they quieted down. After a while, it became totally silent. Something was wrong. I stopped, opened the lid, and discovered they had nearly suffocated.

They quickly revived with the lid open. I cut holes in the lid with my axe. It worked, and we got the puppies home safely.

One time, I came upon a situation where there was a short stretch of open water along a river. Beaver had been coming out to feed on young popple in the nearby woods. There was sign of a lot of activity. It was the beginning of a warm, sunny afternoon, and I figured they would be back out. Instead of setting some traps, I climbed up into a big fallen pine tree. The tree was very old, and was dead when it finally blew over. The few limbs left provided good support. I had an ideal vantage point to look down on everything and the wind was in my favor. I told Sally to hide down below.

Soon, one beaver appeared. It came up on land, and I shot it in the head with my .22 rifle. I told Sally to pull it back out of the way. Another beaver showed up. The same thing happened. Then, another, and another.

I couldn't believe my luck, and didn't want to leave. I stayed up in that tree the entire afternoon and shot a total of seven beaver out of it. Sally pulled each of them off to the side.

Now, I had a big problem. I had seven beaver to skin. Night was coming on and my tent camp was three miles away. Normally, I'd just build a good fire and sit around it for the night. But I'd seen sign of bear out already. I was worried they might find my camp and cause trouble.

I told Sally she had to go back to camp alone and watch things until I could return. She understood perfectly and left. When I came back the next day with seven fresh beaver hides in my pack, there was Sally, waiting for me. She wagged her tail and told me she was glad to see me. I still miss her tremendously. I've had other good dogs since, but there will only be one Sally for me.

My last dog was named Champ. She was a medium-sized, black lab. I had her for five years before she developed distemper. Champ was very good. Her specialty was finding partridge and retrieving them. On a portage, her nose was always working, and she could find any bird around. She developed a technique of charging

them so they would flush up into a nearby tree. She'd sit patiently under the tree, waiting for me to shoot them. Then she'd gently
bring them back.

Jo has always taken good care of our dogs. When I had a dog
team in town, she would go to the grocery store to get scraps of meat
and bones the butcher saved for her. This helped a lot in feeding the
dogs. In later years, she took care of my dog in the house if I was
gone. This happened a lot during the summer when I was off guiding, and sometimes during the winter if the snow was too deep, or it
was too cold for the dog to come with me.

One time, she was home alone with Champ. Jo had baked and
decorated a nice big birthday cake for our granddaughter, Mary. Jo
had put the finished cake on the kitchen table, and left the room.
When she returned, the entire cake was missing; there were no
crumbs, no mess, just an empty plate sitting on the undisturbed
table.

She quickly spied the guilty party. Champ was in her bed, lick-
ing frosting off her whiskers. That is the only time a dog has ever mis-
behaved for either of us. Jo had to bake a second cake and decorate it
again. We all get a good laugh every time we tell the story.

Dogs have been a big part of my life and I can't imagine ever
getting along without them.

14

Near the End of My Life

Here I am in the 1960s, still doing what I have always done: trapping, and guiding fishermen for a living. My personal fishing and hunting also puts food on the table. We bought an electric freezer to store what we can't eat right away. It stays full.

I was nearly accidently killed once while fly fishing at a place called Kimball Meadows with Jack Blackwell, my son-in-law. It was a calm day with no wind. We were using Jack's brother's thirteen-foot Grumman lightweight canoe. Jack was in the bow, I was in the stern, and Champ, my black lab, was on the floor just in front of me. I was slowly paddling along, letting Jack fish out in front of us. Suddenly, out of the corner of my eye, I glimpsed a big snag falling straight at me! I dove forward, pushing the dog ahead, and that snag fell across the back seat of the canoe, right where I had been sitting a moment earlier. It drove the bottom up to the gunnels, and sank us immediately. We were not hurt, and we swam the short distance to shore, towing the canoe. We got up on the boggy land and used both our feet to force the bottom of the canoe back down. We took off our undershirts and ripped rags to stuff in the cracks where the aluminum had split. We managed to paddle back to our vehicle and drove home. Jack had the canoe welded and repaired, but you could always tell that canoe had been through hell. Whatever caused that snag to decide to fall at that moment is beyond me. I guess it wasn't my time to die yet, but that was a close one.

You're never too old to learn something new, and I learned something from a pulp cutter and part-time wolf trapper named Pete Peterson. Pete told me he's learned over the years that the big limbs on jack pine trees located up on ridges always point to the south. He said in cloudy or foggy weather it is a good way to tell directions. I

Alec Boostrom with fly fishing gear. BLACKWELL FAMILY PHOTO

think he's right. Pete also showed me the paste lure he uses for wolves, made by a guy named Herb Lennon in Michigan. It looks and smells similar to the home-made lure I use.

I bought a used, blue Ford pickup with an eight-foot bed. For Christmas, Sister and the kids gave me a very nice topper made by a local guy. I fitted a single box spring and mattress on hinges that would fold up when not in use. I built a drop-down table for my Coleman stove, and a hook in the ceiling for my lantern. This set-up was all I needed for a place to stay while guiding fishermen at the resorts.

Guiding out of McFarland is always eventful. The good walleye fishing is down the Royal River over on North and South Fowl lakes. These lakes are on the Canadian border. It's an hour's boat trip down the river and lakes to South Fowl. Carl Brandt, the resort owner, has learned it works best to move his guests down there by airplane. They leave in the morning, fish during the day, and return in time for the evening cocktail hour.

The pilot's name is Warren LaPlanta. Everyone calls him "Luigi." Luigi has an old Seabee amphibious airplane that seems to be held together with bailing wire. The engine coughs and sputters. It's an ugly-looking thing with the engine in back and a hull that sits low in the water.

Twice the engine has quit while I have been riding in it, and we had to glide back to the lake. Luigi has developed a flying technique at McFarland where he climbs high enough to be able to glide to a lake on any part of the trip.

Everyone has their own favorite story about Luigi. One time he was forced down on Lake Superior, and the US Coast Guard had to tow him in to the Grand Marais harbor. He is still alive and flying, but I'll tell you one thing: Warren LaPlanta is no Ernie Hautala.

In all my years here, I've noticed something unusual about the country around McFarland and elsewhere in far eastern Cook County. It just feels different than anywhere else; not better or worse, just different. The weather seems to behave a little differently there too. Someday, I think they will discover some major mineral, or radioactivity, or something special about this area.

Three cedar paddles carved by Alec for the Hansen Family at Sawbill Canoe Outfitters.
BILL HANSEN

Guiding fishermen at Sawbill Lodge is much quieter than McFarland. It's another walleye lake. There are fewer fish here than on the Fowls, but they are bigger. Jean Raiken is still the owner. She runs a good operation, and I like working for her.

Because this is all federal land, there is only one other business on the lake. Sawbill Canoe Outfitters is located near the campground close to the lodge. Owners Frank and Mary Alice Hansen, and their son, Billy, are nice people. I carved cedar paddles for each member of the family.

Sometime during the 1950s, I quit carrying a .22 rifle. I acquired a 22 High Standard semi-auto pistol with a long barrel and long hand grips with a thumb rest. I built a nice custom leather holster for it, and carry the gun under my left armpit, inside my coat, where it stays clean and dry. I am able to hit what I aim at, and this

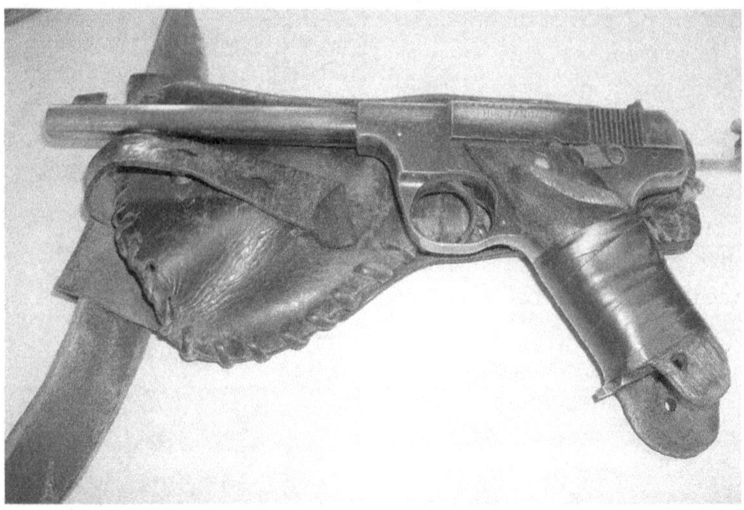

High Standard Model "B" trapline pistol with shoulder holster.
Jack Blackwell

gun does everything I ask of it, from shooting partridge to eat, to squirrels for bait, to killing wolves in my traps.

In the winter of 1962, I snowshoed from the Gunflint Trail down to my Long Island cabin. My purpose for the trip was to carry a load of food to the cabin for the upcoming beaver season. As I got down on Long Island, I kept close to the shore, just like I do in a canoe. As I came around a small point, I spotted two big wolves coming toward me on the ice. I immediately dropped down in the snow with my packsack out in front of me. They hadn't seen me and the slight wind was blowing toward me. I got my pistol out, steadied it on the pack, and let them get close. When they were within range, I started shooting and got both of those wolves. I skinned them at the cabin. When I returned to town I received $70 for the two $35 bounty payments, plus I had the hides. These I tanned and gave to my grandson, Jacky. The bounty money came in handy at this time of the year.

I often use Sawbill Lake as my departure point for trips to the Primitive Area. This includes my fall trips to trap mink. It's important

Alec Boostrom's trout flies. *Note most use deer hair.* JACK BLACKWELL

to understand some things about the timing for mink trapping.

The Minnesota DNR establishes the opening and closing dates for mink season. In an effort to be uniform across the state, they set the opening date to coincide with the mink becoming prime in southern Minnesota. This date occurs about three weeks after our mink get prime. The later date creates big problems for us.

This three-week period is when we are able to move around by canoe prior to freeze up. It is exactly when we need to be out on the lakes covering some country. It is also when our mink will still readily take fish as bait. Waiting until the season officially opens is never a viable option for us in the far north. It forces us to break the law.

In the fall of 1963, I needed to give the Long Island country a rest. That year I built a camp on a lake named Mesaba, a word that means "Giant" in the Ojibwe language. The lake is northwest of Sawbill, way up beyond Kelso Lake. My camp was on the north end of the lake, near the outlet and the long portage down to the Frost River.

I cut logs and built an eight by ten log cabin base about three feet high. On top of this, I constructed a tent frame from poles and covered it with canvas. The place is well-protected from the wind. With an Airtight stove, it was as warm and comfortable as any of my cabins.

I had a beautiful wood and fiberglass canoe that had been modified by my good friend, Art Smith. Art and his brother, Sanford, came from the Arrow Lake country, just over the border in Canada. It's east of Rose Lake. Sanford has passed on and Art now lives in a tiny shack in Grand Marais. He would never talk about why he left Canada, and was careful never to return. Something serious must have happened.

Art was a master in working with wooden canoes. The canoe he cut down for me started as a seventeen-foot Old Town Guide's Model. Art reworked it down to nearly fifteen feet and shortened the height to the gunnels. He shaved off a lot of weight and lightly fiber-glassed it. I used it for trapping mink that fall.

One day, I heard an airplane in the area, but it did not come near me. If it had, I would have tried to hide. The next day, a small Super Cub airplane on floats suddenly appeared. It tried to buzz me and I had a busy time to keep from capsizing. It finally left me alone, but flew over to the next lake where it landed. After a time, I heard it leave and go on to the next lake where it did the same thing.

I investigated, and discovered mink traps set by the occupants of the airplane. Presidential air ban or not, suddenly there was someone trapping in the same area I was. They were obviously not friendly toward me. This was not going to work.

I went back the next two days to one of their trap locations, and hid until the plane and men returned to check it. To my total amazement, I recognized one of the men as a game warden! I remained hidden.

I left my things, paddled out to Sawbill, and went to town. I couldn't turn the men in, because we were all violating trapping regulations prior to the official opening of mink season. I was also breaking Primitive Area rules with construction of my camp and they were violating the presidential air ban.

I went to see Emerson Morris, the county sheriff at the time. Emerson is an ex-commercial pilot and a trapper. He understood exactly what was going on. I told Emerson I was probably going to shoot the plane's engine when the two guys were busy checking their traps, but I would like his advice. Emerson said that was too risky. He said if I was determined to shoot something, he recommended I shoot a couple of holes in their pontoons instead.

I returned to my camp on Mesaba. The plane landed in the area from time to time, but I never got in a position where I felt comfortable enough to shoot at it.

Financially, it was a very poor season for me. I closed up my camp by taking down the pole frame and storing the canvas and stove. Mesaba was still open, but the small lakes had frozen. I cached my canoe and walked out cross-country down to Sawbill. When I snowshoed back to trap beaver in the spring, my canoe was gone. It had to have been stolen by the guys in the plane.

While I was out on Mesaba that fall, Jack and Jacky, who was now a junior in high school, started mink trapping on weekends. They set some traps on streams along the old logging roads between the Greenwood River and what used to be CCC camp #20.

Jack wasn't feeling well and went for a chest X-ray. The following week he went back to the doctor. He had lung cancer. Jack immediately entered the VA hospital in Minneapolis, and was told he had six months to live. He died in five. He was forty-two years old.

I helped my family as best I could over the winter, but I had to trap beaver, which are the main source of my income. In early March, I returned to Mesaba Lake, dug the snow out of my camp and put it back up. I trapped beaver under the ice until nearly the end of the month, when I pulled my traps and snowshoed back out. Jack had just died. I was in time for his funeral.

Sister, Jacky, and I talked. The three of us decided my grandson would not return to high school right away. Instead, he would come back out to Mesaba with me for the month of April. I left right away to get back. Jacky had some beaver traps he needed to pull. A day later, he followed my snowshoe tracks from Sawbill to Mesaba.

We spent the month trapping hard each day and talking each night. I gave him my old Marble skinning knife that I still kept at camp as a spare. I was able to tell him about how it was out here during the old days and told him the stories about my life in this border country.

I also explained many of the things I had learned about trapping, and showed my grandson how I live in harmony with the land. During that month, I was able to demonstrate some of the following lessons:

Have a stove and waterproof shelter during spring break-up and fall freeze-up. You need to be able to dry your clothes after a hard day's work to be ready to go again the next day. I've gotten by without them, but it is much more difficult.

Keep a clean and neat camp. Have one place, well away from your shelter, where you go to the bathroom. Wash your hands morning and night. Wash your dishes thoroughly each day. The only exception is the bottom of your frying pan, which should never be washed, or food will stick to it.

Have two good supplies of matches and store them in separate locations. Always have a good supply of firewood. Get up in the dark and get moving early in the morning. Flour, rice, and beans are good, but you also have to eat meat with them to get the strength you'll need to work hard.

Drink birch bark tea for constipation. Sometimes you can add cedar to it. Boil green popple chips for diarrhea. Boil swamp mint for a cough or any problems with your lungs.

Put balsam pitch on the wound when you cut yourself. You can easily find it by breaking one of the small blisters found everywhere on the bark of the tree. Balsam pitch is a proven remedy to help your skin heal rapidly.

Have great reverence for the land and treat it gently. Be respectful of the animals, just like the Indians are. Make only drowning sets for mink and beaver. Take great care of your fur. Never kill anything you do not need, and use everything from an animal you do have to kill. Never take so many that you deplete their population. Move around from year to year, and give places time to rest.

Spring came very late that year. At the beginning of May, Jacky and I walked on the raised ice back to Sawbill. That summer, I helped build a new house for Sister and her family. It was a precut model, but still took a full summer of work to complete. Life went on.

We still live in our little house on the dead-end street on the west side of Grand Marais. George Plummer and his family are still our neighbors. Directly across from us is the summer home of Birney Quick, a well-known Minneapolis artist. Like

Birney Quick painting of Alec Boostrom. *This painting was given to Jean Boostrom Blackwell by Bernie's widow, Marion, following the death of Alec.* JACK BLACKWELL

me, Birney loves to fly fish for brook trout. His wife, Marion, told Jo that Birney did an oil painting of me from a photo he had. I've never seen it, and wonder what it looks like.

Something happened later that year that had everyone concerned. Minnesota senator Hubert Humphrey wanted to pass a wilderness law. It would affect all of us. In the end, something called the Boundary Waters Canoe Area was created. I didn't know the details, but worried about the changes it might bring for me.

The next year, Jacky reported to me that Pappy Wright from the Forest Service had put up a sign at the end of the new road that had been built to Ball Club Lake. It said you were about to enter the Boundary Waters Canoe Area. Boundary Waters? What was this? We couldn't understand how country thirty miles from the border could be considered boundary waters.

I later learned the one-million-acre wilderness created was called the Boundary Waters Canoe Area, or BWCA for short. It runs from the Canadian border to points thirty miles to the south. The BWCA butts up against the one-million-acre Quetico Provincial Park. So, there are two million acres with similar management.

Jean Raiken retired as county commissioner. Frank Hansen has been elected to take her place. I continue my pattern of trapping and guiding. I do a little more trout fishing. I spend time with my old friend, Charlie Ott, who is still a game warden.

Something completely new came up. The Forest Service wanted to contract with a few local trappers to live-trap fisher. The animals were needed for transplant to national forests in Michigan and Wisconsin. A big population of porcupines down there was eating the bark from pine trees and the trees were dying. Fisher love to eat porcupines, and should solve the problem.

Charlie Ott recommended me. Les Magnus, the forest wildlife biologist, met with me and set up a contract. They would pay one hundred dollars for every live fisher I could deliver. They also supplied the live-traps. For two winters, I became a road trapper; I delivered forty-three live fisher to Les.

I'm sure my success was due to the trapping method I used. I know fisher cannot resist coming to investigate the powerful scent I make. It's a paste lure, created from ground beaver meat, beaver castor, a little bit of skunk urine, and a few other ingredients. It does not smell bad to humans and it also doesn't freeze. Animals readily come to it.

I would place a live-trap on level ground with the back against a good-sized conifer tree. I'd build a modified cubby over and around the trap from dead wood, and cover it with spruce and balsam boughs. The only entrance was through the front door of the live trap. I placed a small amount of scent high in a nearby tree to bring them in. Then I put more of the scent inside the back of the trap. This worked very well.

The program worked so well that Les told me he wrote a scientific paper describing it, and presented the paper at a national meeting of wildlife biologists. He hopes it will inspire biologists elsewhere to consider something like this if they have a similar problem.

By the winter of 1967, I knew there was something seriously wrong with me. My insides weren't right, but I was determined to get back out to my Long Island cabin for spring beaver season. When I die, that's where I wish I could be buried, under a big white pine tree there on the west end. I love the wonderful fragrance of white pine and the special beauty of that place. Out there I am content and completely at peace. It is my real home.

I told Charlie Ott where I was going and showed him the location of my cabin on a map. Charlie has now been a game warden for forty-two years, and we've been friends for most of that time. Charlie said Bob Hodge, the game warden from Ely who flew the state plane, intended to come over to patrol with him. It would be sometime in the spring. They would try to check on me.

By this time, Jacky was attending college in Duluth, but he came home on some weekends. He and Buck Smith's boy, Stanley, took me on snowmobiles down the Rib Lake Trail. We crossed the lake and went down to the bay on the southwest end that I know so well. I didn't try to take the snowmobiles any farther and said goodbye to the boys.

I brought six light packsacks; none of them weighed more than twenty-five pounds. Over the next few days, I carried them one at a time down to Long Island. I trapped beaver as I had always done, but things were not right. When I went to the bathroom I had blood in my stools.

One day I snowshoed up to my cabin and spotted ski tracks from an airplane on the ice. Charlie had been there to check on me, and he had left a nice note. I appreciated this, because if I had been really sick it would have been welcome help.

When the season was over, I carried my packsack of beaver hides and walked out to the Gunflint Trail. It was a difficult trip. The Cross River was running high and was impossible to cross on foot. Any ice left on the lakes was not safe to walk on. I finally found a big spruce tree growing right near the river. It took an hour with my axe, but I managed to fell it across the river. I was able to safely cross on it.

Once I got home, I went to the doctor and was diagnosed with colon cancer. They sent me to Duluth for an operation, after which I returned home.

I am grateful for Jo. She's taken good care of me. She has not had an easy life and she has never complained. I'm spending this summer with my family. I am at peace looking back at my life in the woods, and have good feelings as I get ready to die.

EPILOGUE

Alec Boostrom closed his eyes and died peacefully on August 23, 1967. He is buried in the old section of the Chippewa City cemetery, east of Grand Marais.

Today, the Boundary Waters Canoe Area Wilderness is just as spectacular and still very similar to how it looked when Alec first saw it over one hundred years ago. It is in another period of forest fires, and the cycle of life goes on. Alec must be pleased.

Alec's cabins are gone. His Long Island cabin site cannot even be located. A dense forest of balsam has grown so thick it is nearly impossible to walk through. The big white pine tree he so loved still stands on the west end of the lake. At his Frost River cabin, beaver built a dam and flooded the spruce swamp that was located next to the cabin. The beaver moved out, the dead trees have fallen, and the former spruce swamp is now a big, grassy area. An old ice chisel has been pushed into the ground and stands guard over the cabin remains, with parts of the log walls still visible. The big boulder remains perched on the ledge above the cabin. Harry Hummitch's cabin on Crocodile is also gone. If you know where to look, a few remnants of the cabin and his cook stove can still be found.

Change is continuous, even in wilderness. In a short time, nothing will indicate where Alec's cabins stood and no evidence will be left to remind us of the men who lived at these places and what they experienced. However, Alec's stories remain. It is good that he told them and they are now recorded.

Jack Blackwell, 2016

LIST OF HISTORICAL RECORDS

Beatty, Leslie R. "A Forest Ranger's Diary, Part XXXI." Minnesota Conservation Volunteer Magazine. Minnesota Department of Natural Resources, St. Paul. January–February, 1968.

"A Forest Ranger's Diary, Part XXVII." Minnesota Conservation Volunteer Magazine. Minnesota Department of Natural Resources, St. Paul. July–August, 1967.

"A Forest Ranger's Diary, Part XXVI." Minnesota Conservation Volunteer Magazine. Minnesota Department of Natural Resources, St. Paul. January–February, 1967.

Blackwell, Billy. Taped Interview with Charlie Cook. April 3, 1997.

Blackwell, Faith. Papa Was a Printer. New York: Vantage Press, 1975.

Brickner, Joseph. "A Pioneer Game Warden." Minnesota Conservation Volunteer Magazine. Minnesota Department of Natural Resources, St. Paul. November–December, 1960.

Carey, Bob, and Jack Hautala. Bush Pilots, Legends of the Old and Bold. Cambridge, MN: Adventure Publications, Inc. 2003.

Coatsworth, Emerson S. The Indians of Quetico. Published for the Quetico Foundation by University of Toronto Press. 1957.

Cook County Historical Society. Faces and Places II. Second Edition. Grand Marais: The Print Shop. 2011.

Pioneer Faces and Places. Superior, WI: Arrowhead Printing. 1979.

Cook County News-Herald. "Arrest by Charlie Boostrom of Joseph Chosa and man named Roy for trapping 24 beaver and 3 muskrats." November 8, 1923.

"Arrest by game warden George Mayhew of Swamper Cariboo and Leonce Zimmerman for trapping beaver." June 26, 1924.

Hangartner, Elizabeth Zimmerman. "Letter to New Ulm's Diamond Jubilee and Homecoming regarding the New Ulm Massacre." Beaver Bay, MN. 1929.

Hautala, Jack. Personal Interview with the author. October 11, 2014.

Helland, John. "Chronology of Historical Actions for Boundary Waters Canoe Area Wilderness within Minnesota's Superior National Forest." Information Brief. Minnesota House of Representatives, Research Department, St. Paul. 2004.

Hess, Jeffrey. "National Register of Historic Places Inventory – Nomination Form." Clearwater Lodge. 1985.

Kerfoot, Justine. Gunflint, Reflections on the Trail. Minneapolis: University of Minnesota Press. 1991.

Gunflint, The Trail, The People, The Stories. Cambridge, MN: Adventure Publications, Inc. 2003.

Lund, Duane R. Our Historic Boundary Waters. Staples, MN: Nordell Graphic Communications, Inc. 1980.

Magie, Bill. A Wonderful Country. Edited by David Olesen. Ashland, WI: The Sigurd Olson Environmental Institute. 1981.

Members of the Potomac Corral of the Westerners. Great Western Indian Fights, the Defining Battles. New York: MJF Books, Fine Communications. 1960.

Ogren, Beatrice Flaaten. Gunflint Trail Blazers, the Story of Charlie and Petra Boostrom. Grand Marais, MN: Cook County Historical Society. 1985.

Peruniak, Shirley. Quetico Provincial Park, An Illustrated History. Atikokan, Ontario: Friends of Quetico Park. 2000.

Powell, Betsy. Betsy and Saganaga. Cambridge, MN: Adventure Publications, Inc. 2004.

Raff, LeRoy. "Reminiscences of Early Days in Cook County, recalled by Sam Zimmerman, Sr." Cook County News-Herald. July 5, 1934.

Raff, Willis H. "Pioneers in the Wilderness." Cook County Historical Society. Sauk Rapids, MN: Sentinel Printing Co. 1981.

"Law and Order in the Wilderness." Cook County Historical Society, Sauk Rapids, MN: Sentinel Printing Co. 1982.

Skoog, Betty Powell, with Justine Kerfoot. A Life in Two Worlds. Lake Nebagamon, WI: Paper Moon Publishing. 1996.

Stenlund, Milton H. "Wildlife Refuges in the Superior." Minnesota Conservation Volunteer Magazine. Minnesota Department of Natural Resources, St. Paul. November–December, 1958.

Toftey, Ade. Typed notes from taped audio interview with old timers J.A. Blackwell and Matt Johnson.

Vizenor, Gerald Robert. The People Named the Chippewa. Minneapolis: University of Minnesota Press. 1984.

Williams, Bronwyn W., Jonathan H. Gilbert, and Patrick A. Zollner. Historical Perspective on the Reintroduction of Fisher and Pine Marten in Wisconsin and Michigan. U.S. Department of Agriculture Forest Service, Northern Research Station. General Technical Report NRS-5. 2007.

Wolff Jr., Julius F. "Our Pioneer Game Wardens." Minnesota Conservation Volunteer Magazine. Minnesota Department of Natural Resources, St. Paul. November–December, 1980.

"Some Major Forest Fires in the Sawbill Country." Minnesota History Magazine. Minnesota Historical Society, St. Paul. December, 1958.

Hot Fur, RENDEVOUS, Selected Papers of the Fourth North American Fur Trade Conference in 1981. North American Fur Trade Conference, St. Paul. 1984.

Wright-Peterson, Ralph. Benny Ambrose, Life in the Boundary Waters. Minnesota Historical Society, St. Paul. 1994.

ABOUT THE AUTHOR

Jack Blackwell is Alec Boostrom's grandson. Jack was born and raised in northern Minnesota where he learned to trap, hunt, fish, and canoe in the Boundary Waters with his father and grandfathers. He is referred to as "Jacky" in this book.

Blackwell retired from the US Forest Service after a forty-year career. He went on to work for the Rocky Mountain Elk Foundation. Today, he and his wife, Pat, and their black Lab, Sally, live at an airport community on the Snake River in southern Idaho. Their son, Jack, is a park ranger for the State of Alaska.

Cover photo: Alec Boostrom preparing to leave family farm in Milaca. BOOSTROM FAMILY

Back cover photo: Color painting of Alec Boostrom by well-known Minneapolis artist, Bernie Quick. JACK BLACKWELL

CPSIA information can be obtained
at www.ICGtesting.com
Printed in the USA
LVHW03s1017170718
584000LV00002B/3/P